Henrietta Branford grew up in the New Forest with "gun dogs, blood sports and a selection of extremely good old books. My father taught me a great deal about animals from a shooting and fishing perspective. It was a wonderfully accurate and unsentimental way to learn." She had a variety of jobs before coming to writing at the age of forty, starting with a regular column in a local newspaper and then moving on to children's fiction. Among her many books are *Dipper's Island, White Wolf* and three stories about Dimanche Diller, the first of which, *Dimanche Diller in Danger,* won the Smarties Book Prize. *Fire, Bed and Bone* won the Guardian Children's Fiction Award and a Smarties Book Prize Bronze Award, as well as being Highly Commended for the Carnegie Medal. Henrietta Branford died in April 1999.

Books by the same author

The Fated Sky

White Wolf

For younger readers

Dimanche Diller

Dimanche Diller in Danger

Dimanche Diller at Sea

Dipper's Island

Spacebaby

Picture books

Birdo

Someone Somewhere

FIRE, BED AND BONE

HENRIETTA BRANFORD

WALKER BOOKS
AND SUBSIDIARIES
LONDON • BOSTON • SYDNEY

First published 1997 by Walker Books Ltd
87 Vauxhall Walk, London SE11 5HJ

This edition published 2002

6 8 10 9 7 5

This book has been typeset in Cochin

Printed and bound in Great Britain by
Cox & Wyman Ltd, Reading, Berkshire

British Library Cataloguing in Publication Data:
a catalogue record for this book is
available from the British Library

ISBN 0-7445-9049-3

For my father

Chapter One

The wolves came down to the farm last night. They spoke to me of freedom.

I lay by the last of the fire with my four feet turned towards the embers and the last of the heat warming my belly. I did not listen to the wolf talk. This is no time to think of freedom.

Tomorrow, in the morning, I will choose the place. Out in the byre, where the bedding is deep and the children cannot find me.

My back aches from the pull of my belly. However long I lap from the cold cattle trough I am still thirsty. I think tomorrow is the day.

I rest. The fire ticks. Grindecobbe grunts in her stall. Humble creeps in through the window and curls beside me, soft as smoke.

I can smell mouse on her. She has eaten, and come in to the fire for the warmth.

Rufus snores on his pallet of straw. Comfort, his wife, lies curled around him, dreaming. Down by their feet the children cough and fidget in their sleep, as children do. Only Alice, the baby, is awake. Only she hears, with me and Humble, the wild song of the wolves.

I heave my belly up and hobble on splayed feet to stand beside the cradle. Alice reaches her small, red fist towards my ear and smiles. She does not fear the wolves. Their voices come to her from far outside the house, which is the only world she knows.

Thin, frail, far off and going further, their call wavers back from where the snow lies deep under the pine trees. The grey rock pushes like bone through the cold hide of the earth and the moon hangs over all.

I know the world beyond the house. I know Rufus's byre. I know Joan's house, which stands beside the village field. I know all the village. I know the Great House barn and sheep pens; I know the Great House fields. I know every small place where oats and beans and barley grow.

I know where the rabbits creep out from their burrows. I know where the wicked wildcat leaves her stink on the grass as she passes. I know where foxes hunt, where deer step out on fragile legs to graze. I know where the wild boar roots and where the great bear nurses. I know where the little grey bear with the striped face digs for bluebell bulbs in springtime, when the woods are full of hatchlings that fall into your mouth, dusted with down, and the rabbits on the bank are slow and sleek and foolish.

I am a creature of several worlds. I know the house and the village and have my place in both. I know the pasture land beyond the great field. I know the wildwood. I know the wetlands all along the river, where every green leaf that you step on has a different smell. I know the high, dry heath.

Soon now I shall climb into the bracken stack next to the medlars that sit in rows, skins wrinkling while they ripen and decay. I'll make a bed there, like the soft bed Rufus made for Comfort at the time of Alice's birth.

I shall not groan, as Comfort did, nor beg Rufus to rub my back. I shall push and wait and push again, three, four, maybe five times.

Move over, Humble, let me uncoil my aching back.

Chapter Two

"Old bitch looks ready to drop her pups."

That's Rufus talking. He bends down and rubs his hard hand down from the base of my skull to the root of my tail. Again. Again.

Comfort looks my way and smiles. "I wonder where she'll hide this time? Why won't she stay beside the fire, Rufus?"

"She knows what's best for her."

Rufus is a good man. When Comfort hollered from the pain of the baby before Alice, he put his weight behind her and his strength and his voice, put everything he could behind her, tried his best to coax that child out.

In the end he ran for help. I stayed with Comfort while he went for Ede. They always go for Ede when they need help of this kind.

The child was out and dead before they got

back. There was a smell of blood. Comfort lay very still. Her twins, Wat and Will, sat by the fire with their fingers in their mouths, not looking. The new one didn't move, not even to draw breath.

Poor Comfort. That was the year two of mine were born blind. Rufus took them. I bit his thumb near to the bone.

Next year came sweet Alice.

"Give the old dog a dish of milk, Rufus."

Rufus shook his head. "Do you think I'm a rich man, Comfort, to feed my dog on milk? Not I. I work for what I get."

Comfort smiled, because he had already lifted the crock that holds the milk down off the windowsill.

"And so do I," she said. "And so does the old dog. That's the best hunting dog we've ever had. Best in the village and you know it. Everybody knows it. She does you credit, Rufus."

Rufus poured my milk.

"Wolves were close round the farm last night, Comfort. I saw their tracks in the snow when I went out this morning. It's good that we mended the Great House sheep pen."

"I will keep the boys close by until the snow lifts."

"Wolves won't take a child. Not while there's lambs to take."

Comfort did not reply. She disagrees with Rufus on the matter of what wolves will and will not take. And so do I. Only a wolf knows what a wolf wants.

I slipped away from the fire while they were talking, and made my way across the yard to the byre. There is more snow to fall. It will overlay my footprints.

It was hard work, to drag my belly up the wooden steps and into the bracken Rufus cuts for bedding. The chickens squawked each time I slipped; the goat watched with those yellow eyes of hers. They winter in the byre with the sheep. Grindecobbe lives indoors with us.

I pushed in under the wooden platform where they store the medlars. The place was perfect. Dark, hidden, high. Not safe. Nothing is safe. But easy to defend.

I could hear the sheep moving down below, and the goat fidgeting. I smelled the bracken. Clean. Dry. I turned around and around, treading my nest. As I lay down, satisfied, the pit of my belly started to tighten.

One of the hens has flown up here to watch me. Her fierce round eye stares at me and her head tilts to one side. A long, slow cluck escapes her throat. Hens know how to hatch eggs and how to keep a clutch of chicks warm under wing and how to scratch for food, but they are ignorant of anything beyond their own concerns.

Oof!

Hens do very well as hens. They are not stupid. But they are no good at any but hens' business. Sheep are the same. There are two in the stall below me waiting to lamb. I hear them now; they grind their jaws from side to side, working the cud.

Horses, now—

Oof!

Horses are different. Mullein the Great House horse is a good-hearted beast, patient and strong and brave.

Oof!

Welcome, my sweet. Soft yellow gold, like me.

Burdock the ox is strong, but foolish. He can pull the plough and take the cart to market. But I do not like him.

Oof!

Welcome, damp wriggler. Lie still beside your sister.

There'll be no market while the snow blocks the road. There'll be no coming and no going. Burdock will champ in his stall.

Oof!

Welcome. Are you the last and latest, small one, smudged smidgen of a puppy?

I think so.

Yes. Just three.

One golden brown. One black, like Swart, your father. One smudged. Two dogs and a bitch. Lie still and let me clean you. Oh, the sweet, soft smallness of you under my tongue. Suckle, and I'll name you.

Squill, my little black dog, Swart's son. Your nose shines like a wet black leaf. Parsnip, small daughter, yellow like me. Little two-colour fellow, I shall call you Fleabane.

Go, hen. You've seen them now. Go down and tell your sisters that my pups are born. Call out the news. Let Swart hear it too, over the hills.

Squill, your small teeth prick like pine needles. Stop that, Parsnip, and let your brother Fleabane feed beside you.

Night comes again. Snowfall and darkness and the quiet wind. I'll make a circle round my pups, and sleep.

Chapter Three

Days and nights we stayed up in the bracken pile, curled round one another, while I gave suck and licked and settled squabbles. They fed and slept and fed and squabbled and I watched their small, sleek bodies plumping up with milk. Their eyes were shut, their small heads pushed into my flank, muzzles butting, jaws working hard in the rhythm of life, which is, at first, no more than suck and swallow.

I went down by night to drink at the trough. Comfort put bread and milk for me inside the byre door, and now and then a bone. She knew where I was, though she pretended not to.

Then the cold bit hard, the last cold of

winter, and the trough froze solid right down to the bottom. The hens stuck their feathers up and the goat complained. Only the sheep seemed not to feel it.

No more snow fell, but that which lay about the yard rang like iron under Rufus's leather boots. Frost silvered the hills and made the trees shine. Even the bracken where we lay grew a white bloom, and crackled.

Fleabane, my smallest, began to whine and shiver, so I picked him up and bumped him, dangling from my jaws, down to the ground and across the yard. I scratched at the door till Comfort let me in. I put Fleabane down under Comfort's stool, told him to stay, and went back to fetch Parsnip and then Squill.

Rufus found an old sheepskin that was badly cured and stank. He put it down on the earth floor for us and there we lay, wrapped round about with warmth and woodsmoke. He set up a wooden board so Grindecobbe could not reach the puppies if she blundered through from her stall.

It was a long, cold spring. I lay by the fire with my puppies and I heard much talk. Rufus liked to talk and Comfort liked to listen. They were close and comfortable.

"There is trouble coming," Rufus said one

evening. He was carving a spoon for Alice. "It follows from the great plague, Comfort, as flies follow rubbish to the midden."

"How so, Rufus?"

"The plague killed so many, Comfort, labour was scarce, good fields were left untilled. Poor folk like us began to know our worth and ask for better wages. That angered King Edward, our king's father. When the strong grow angry, Comfort, the weak will suffer."

Rufus was young, just married to his first wife, when the great plague came to the village. Comfort was not yet born.

"My first wife, Joan, and our child, Clary, both took ill at the start and died within a week. Next died my father. After him my mother. I lost my brother too, who was a shepherd, and his wife and all their children. More than half the village died."

"What did you do, Rufus?" Comfort would ask. Stories so full of sorrow need retelling.

"I ran off to the wildwood with two other lads."

"You left the village, Rufus, and your home?"

"Best go, we told each other, while yet we lived. But it wasn't fear of death that drove us, Comfort. It was the lonely quiet of the village with all our people gone. Houses empty. Doors banging. Fires out. No smoke rising. Starving dogs dragging themselves from door to door. Beasts out on the meadow lowing to be milked. Crops in the fields and nobody to harvest them. Thieves and murderers on every road and highway. Nobody even in the church. Priest died early on. And the next one, sent to us by the Lord Bishop, soon ran off. Comfort, it felt like the end of the world."

"Tell me how it was, out in the wildwood, Rufus."

"Clean and green, Comfort. Clean and green. And we stayed there, hunting King Edward's deer and burning King Edward's firewood, through five summers and four winters."

"Did you meet outlaws, Rufus? And wild men? And witches?"

Comfort loved stories.

I lay beside the fire, with Squill and Parsnip and Fleabane suckling in a row, or sleeping, or squeaking and nuzzling one another. I loved to hear Rufus's slow voice.

"After the worst of the plague was gone, I came back to the village. That was a bad time, Comfort. The plague had carried off half the people. The King laid new laws on those who were left, making life harder even than God had made it. The plague came back each year and killed a few more people. I mended my father's roof and tended my father's field and lived alone as best I could. Till you passed by my door."

Next came the part of the story that was Comfort's favourite: how Rufus couldn't rest until he found out who she was and where she came from, how he courted her, how everybody said he was too old for her and her own father said she needn't wed him if she didn't want to, although his house was fine and his field fertile; and how she said she would; and how she did.

I lay by the fire and listened. Next they spoke about a poor preacher who had come to the village last summer. The priest wouldn't let him in the church, so he spoke out under the trees, at the edge of the wood. I remembered it myself, because of the preacher's dog.

It was a summer evening, hot and dry and still. The leaves hung quiet on the trees, the grass was burned and bleached; it crackled when you stepped on it.

Rufus and Comfort sat on the hard earth, their brown faces smeared with sweat and dirt from the long day's labour. They had worked all hours cutting hay for the Great House and had their own small crop to fetch in later. Now they were thankful to put down their long scythes and rest their aching shoulders and feel their swollen feet come back to life as the day's weight was taken from them.

The younger people would rather have been dancing, but they listened. Out on the fringes of the groups, we dogs drowsed, and scratched for fleas.

"Do you believe," the preacher asked, "that God made the poor to be the servants of the rich?"

Nobody answered. The preacher's dog caught a flea, cracked it between his teeth, and glanced up at his master.

"What did He make Adam? Rich man? Poor man?"

Still nobody answered.

"I will tell you," the preacher said. "I will tell you what the Bible says about it."

The preacher's dog shut his eyes. He'd heard it all before.

"The Bible says that God told Adam he must sweat to eat. Do you see my Lord Bishop sweat for what he eats? Do you see the Lord of the Manor, whose harvest you are bringing in just now, sweat for what is laid upon his table? Or do you rather sweat to lay it there?"

"It's our sweat lays his table," Rufus said. "And fills the Church's money box."

Rufus would always speak his mind.

The preacher nodded. "Adam planted oats and beans and barley, just as you do. He pastured his cows, he led his sheep onto the hills to graze. God gave no serf to Adam to till his field. God gave no shepherd to Adam to pasture his flocks. God gave Adam a strong back and told him to get on with it."

"Adam was a sinner," Will Cudweed, the miller, said. "Any fool knows that." He was standing behind the others, with his dog Avens cringing behind him on the end of a cord.

Beton, the miller's wife, sat away on her own. Beton was Comfort's sister but she had few friends in the village. Too many people feared her husband. She often bore the marks of his bad temper herself. That evening, I remember, she had a bruise on her cheekbone, just under her eye.

"Adam was that. Like you and me," the preacher granted. "But tell me, Miller, who did God send, to save us all from Adam's sins? Was it a king?"

The miller shook his head.

"A baron, then? A knight? A handsome miller, maybe, with a sack of coin to his name?"

A chuckle rippled round the crowd. The miller scowled and jerked at Avens's cord.

"God sent a carpenter, as you should know,

Sir Miller. Someone who works for what he gets."

One or two people nodded.

"Why should the rich folk ride on your bent backs? Is that the way God made the world? There's nothing in the Bible says so!" The preacher sighed and looked around. "As you would know," he said, more quietly, "if you were let to read it."

The moon rose and the young people slipped away into the wood and the crowd dwindled down to half a dozen men and women, drinking in the preacher's words. Rufus and Comfort were with them.

My eyes closed and I dreamed of a young rabbit, jinking ahead of me over close-cropped grass, fast, but not fast enough. I seemed to feel the snap of my teeth on the small bones of its neck and its good weight dangling from my jaws; to taste the rich, moist flavour of it slipping down my throat. It was a good dream, but something woke me from it.

The preacher's dog, with his nose in my ear. We slipped away under the trees to look for wood mice. But there was a bad smell under the trees, a smell of sickness and sorrow and secrets. At first we saw only black shadows and white stipples of moonlight and the shift and sift of leaves. Then something moved, deep in the wood, and we noticed a man, lapped in shadow, muffled up in rags, leaning against a tree. He spat and wiped his forehead. His head moved slightly as he counted the men and women who still listened to the preacher.

My neck bristled and I jumped up, growling. I glanced at the preacher's dog and saw that his hackles were rising too. When I looked back, the rag man was gone.

Some weeks later, news came that the preacher was taken by the Lord Bishop's men and locked up for speaking sacrilege. I wondered if his dog was locked up with him.

"Church rules us with a hard rod, Comfort," Rufus said when he heard of it.

"That preacher said no more than what is true," Comfort agreed. "But no doubt our priest was angry. He would have us listen only to himself, inside the church, and not to any poor preacher."

The next spring, when two men knocked on our door seeking shelter and speaking words of freedom, Rufus and Comfort let them in, and listened. They were poor people, moving by night when the moon gave enough light, keeping to woods and wild places by day. They spoke in whispers and when they'd finished whispering, they left.

That was the busy time of year, with

ploughing and spring sowing every day. Rufus pulled a bush harrow made of blackthorn up and down his strip of land, while Comfort planted peas and beans.

But the whisperers came back, and others like them. They came, and went, and whispered.

"Orderic's been taken. And Henry and Ralph."

"Tell John of Stourvale not to trust John Merriman."

"Tell Thomas Kemp to go to Rother with all speed and seek there Rannulf Burgate and his wife Alyssum."

"Send to Flettwood on the Ouse. Tell them John Ball is taken. Tell them not to pay their taxes."

"Thomas de Bampton's men have lost their heads and his house is burned."

"Wat Tyler will lead us."

"We march on London."

"Be ready, when you get the signal:

John Ball
Greeteth you all
And doth you to understand
He hath rung your bell
Now with right and might
Will and skill
God speed every dell!"

Every man who came to Rufus's house talked of rebellion. They wanted just laws and fair wages and most of all an end to serfdom. Wild talk. Wolf talk. Comfort and Rufus listened. When the signal came, they passed it on to those they trusted in the village. Only to those few whom it was safe to tell. Or so they thought.

The next knock at the door brought the priest and the soldiers and death.

Chapter Four

The soldiers burst in, cursed Rufus for his slowness, pushed Comfort up against the wall and tied her hands, beat Rufus, shouted at the twins to hold their noise, and kicked me clear across the room.

The priest watched it all with a smile on his face. Behind him stood Will Cudweed the miller. Grindecobbe ran out and bit him on the leg. She's not a bad sow, Grindecobbe.

Comfort looked back at me as they pulled her away. I met her gaze and told her as clearly as I could that I would guard her children. Rufus could not see. There was blood running down into his eyes.

I knew the children would not be safe unless I could get them away. I carried my own three across the yard and up into the bracken stack and told Squill, who was the least obedient of the three, that I would bite his tail off if he moved.

Wat and Will had crept behind Grindecobbe's stall when first the soldiers came. They seemed likely to stay there, but I was afraid for Alice, who lay howling in her cradle. Some men will kill a baby just to quiet her. She was still tightly bundled up inside her shawl against the cold and I picked her up easily, for all her struggling, holding the folds of wool between my teeth. She stopped howling, more from surprise than any other reason I expect, and let me nudge her in beside her brothers. She never feared me, that child. Wat leaned out and took her.

Humble watched from the windowsill, ready to run. Cats have no courage. I snapped at her to show my scorn, and ran out.

I ran over the hill to Ede and scratched at her door. I scratched and whined and whimpered and scratched and whined again, until at last I saw her pull back the hide that hung across her window and peep out. She knew enough of what was in the air to guess that my coming, all alone, meant trouble.

I licked her hand and led her to the door. She shook her head. I nudged and nuzzled till she fetched her shawl, pulled on her boots, and followed me out into the night. I brought her to our door, which still stood open, as the soldiers had left it, letting the cool air swill round inside the room like water in a bucket.

She crossed herself, straightened her bent back, and walked into the dark room. There was no light. There was no sound.

I feared the soldiers had been back and that I was too late, but when I stuck my nose round the end of Grindecobbe's stall, Wat's fat, grubby hand clutched my fur, and he began to cry.

The noise of his crying, and his brother Will's, and Alice's too, told Ede all that she needed to know. She tied Alice to her back. She took as much as she could carry from the room – a sack of beans, two hens, a pile of flax Comfort was drying. She told Wat and Will to take the flour crock between them, patted my head, and left.

I threw myself across the room and up into the loft. Fleabane lay alone in the bracken, crying. There was a rank stench of cat all round him. Not Humble's smell. The stronger smell of *wildcat*. I put my nose down and ran, sucking up catsmell, out across the yard, up the field and into the wood. I knew Parsnip and Squill were dead. They would have died before she took them from the loft.

I knew I could not get them back. I just wanted to kill her. I heard her brats mewing from a hollow high up in a tree trunk and I wanted to kill them too. I clawed at the bark of the tree. I sat underneath it and howled. When I had howled out all my anger I went back to Fleabane in the loft.

He was hungry by then, and lonely and very scared. I fed him and washed him and let him sleep a little, but I knew we could not stay. The wildcat would be back as soon as I left Fleabane on his own again. And if she was not, the soldiers might be. Anyone, seeing the place empty, might move in. If they had dogs of their own already, as most people do, they might not want me or Fleabane. What people do not want they usually destroy.

When Fleabane had slept a little and I was rested too, I took the soft folds of his scruff between my teeth and carried him off from the house that had been home for all my life, and out into the wild world, where people do not go. It seemed the only safe thing I could do.

Chapter Five

We were not, nor would ever be, truly wild. I had known fireside, bed and bone, Rufus's pat and his soft look. All of my life up till then had been lived in the village. But still I was no hand-fed house dog. I knew what to do and how to do it. And the summer had started, which brings easy living.

I carried Fleabane, curled limp from my jaws, bouncing and swinging up the hill above the village. Halfway to the top there was a pile of rocks that jutted out from under an earth mound. It smelled a bit of fox, but there were none there at that time. I crept in underneath the rocks, with Fleabane still held safely in my jaws. A passage led back right inside the mound. There was more rock in there and dry, white bones and a spear and helmet with the skull still inside it, all so old that not the faintest whiff of people hung about them.

There was a little pile of soft ash near the helmet. Something had burned there, long ago. It made a smooth bed for my Fleabane, and I laid him down. He wanted me to stay with him, but I was hungry.

There was a rabbit warren down at the bottom of the hill, on Great House land. Dawn was coming, when the rabbits would come out to crop and nibble.

I caught one, snapped its neck, and felt its warm flesh and blood bringing me life and strength. I caught another one and carried it back to my new home. I let Fleabane nose its fur, though he was too young to eat it.

When I had fed and washed Fleabane, I left him sleeping and went to lie in the mouth of our den. It was a strange and lonely feeling, watching the sun come up, hearing the birds wake, seeing the cows at pasture below.

Towards midday I saw what I'd been watching for. A group of soldiers, with four prisoners between them. Rufus and Comfort and two neighbours. Ede was not with them. Wat and Will and Alice might still be safe with her.

I woke Fleabane and told him I must go

away, but not for long, and that he must stay in the lair and not for any reason put his small brown nose outside it. There was still one rabbit leg for him to play with.

I wanted to run straight to Rufus, to hear his voice, to feel his hand on my head, to lick Comfort's brown hand. But I feared the soldiers. So I sneaked along, belly to the ground, dodging behind bushes, keeping low in ditches. Rufus did not see me. If he had seen me and called I would have run to him.

The soldiers took him to the stables in the yard of the Great House and pushed him and Comfort and the other two, all four into one stall. They shut and locked the doors behind them. One soldier stood outside.

The priest came and gabbled some rigmarole outside the stable door. I doubt if they could hear him inside. He spoke of treason and rebellion and King Richard's men. He spoke of law courts and execution. Beton, the miller's wife, watched with tears running down her face.

There is an old dog, Filbert, in the Great House yard, and I knew that he would watch the stable and bring me news, so I went back to Fleabane.

On the way I saw Humble, hunting along the edge of the village. She spat at me. She has no loyalty at all.

Chapter Six

Fleabane and I continued in the same den through the early summer and I began to teach him how to hunt. We started with nestlings and young rabbits.

Rufus always loved to watch me teach a young dog. People would beg him for a pup of mine. Will Cudweed offered to grind our corn free for one season in exchange for two strong pups of mine, but Rufus wouldn't trade.

"That man would beat the sense out of the best dog in England," he told Comfort. "I'm blowed if he's beating it out of any dog of mine, corn or no corn."

Will Cudweed was angry, very. But Rufus wouldn't entertain him.

Fleabane's first proper kill, made on his own without my help, was a leveret. Grown hares can run like the wind, but a leveret will crouch in the form where its mother leaves it and is easy meat. Still, this one was in long grass and Fleabane did well to find it. I let him eat it all.

After that there was no stopping him. He learned to stalk and pounce and snap the spine of his prey with one flick of his jaws. He learned all the joy of finding, chasing, catching, from the first faint scent of prey to the hot salt taste of blood, the snap and speed and triumph of the kill.

He was a patient little dog right from the start, careful and thorough, but quick when speed was called for. I never had to show him the same skill twice; he would pick it up the first time, practise it, perfect it.

His stalk was excellent. He could press his belly to the ground and crawl on his ribcage like a snake. He could cross open ground better than dogs twice his age.

I taught him to know all the smells a hunter needs. He could tell hare from rabbit easily and plan his hunt accordingly. He could tell grouse from partridge, woodcock from snipe; he even knew his deer – buck from doe and both from fawn. I taught him that in case we might fall in with other dogs and hunt packwise sometime.

I taught him all I knew and he has never once disgraced me.

By day we kept out of the village, but sometimes at night I would leave Fleabane snoring in our den and creep down to Filbert in the Great House yard, to sniff and snuff outside the stable door.

As days and nights went by, the smell got very bad and I knew that those inside were suffering. They had been there since spring, and it was summer now. People are not fastidious, like dogs, but they do not like to lie in their own muck.

One night Filbert took me round to the back of the stables and showed me a gap between the planks.

I put my eye to the chink and looked through. Four figures slumped against the walls, facing inwards. They sat on filthy straw, wet with their excrement. Chains held them to the walls. Their faces looked blank, even Rufus's. Their skins were grey under many layers of dirt. Their hair was lank and greasy. Comfort's eyes were closed in wretched sleep. Rufus stared at his bare feet.

I whined a little whine and yipped, but quietly. Rufus looked up. He knew at once that it was me and tried to reach the part of the wall where I was waiting, nose to chink, but his chain would not reach so far.

"Comfort," he croaked. "Wake up, Comfort,

the old dog's here. She's over by the wall there! I cannot go. You try if you can reach her."

Comfort woke, crawled over the foul straw and laid her cheek against the rough wood, calling me. She poked one finger through the chink and scratched behind my ear. She wept.

Just then a soldier strolled into the yard. His heavy boots clumped on the cobblestones and the iron on the bottom of his pike struck sparks.

I ran off back to Fleabane in our lair, but the stench of Rufus's despair and Comfort's misery ran with me and I could neither shake it off my pelt, nor roll it off, nor sneeze it from my nose.

The next night I took Fleabane with me and we went to Ede's house. Oh, it was fine and good to see young Wat and Will again, and best of all to see my Alice.

"You can't stay here, old dog," Ede scolded. "And nor can that puppy of yours neither. I can't feed another mouth, never mind two more. Go on out!"

But all the same she let us in to sniff and snuff the children. Will and Wat were over-joyed to see me, and delighted with how big Fleabane had grown. Alice pulled my tail and tried to gum my ear.

I nosed under Ede's table for scraps but found instead Alice's little hat. It smelled so sweetly of her that I snatched it up. Ede scolded me and off I ran with Fleabane behind me, across the big meadow to the Great House yard.

Filbert, the Great House dog, met us outside the yard wall and told us not to go inside. Soldiers were there and the priest and the Lord of the Great House with his steward, the reeve. Someone had died inside the stable.

I watched from outside the gate as the soldiers pulled a body out. They took off his chains and laid him on a hurdle and two of them dragged him off to bury him behind the midden tip.

The other three were pulled out next, alive. Their straw was taken out and fresh straw thrown inside. Then they were shoved back in, the door was bolted and everybody went away.

I knew the dead man. He kept his goats in much the same state he himself had suffered as a prisoner. I did not care about him either way. Rufus was living. Comfort too. That was what I cared about.

When it was safe and the thin moon was nosing up over the yard wall and the shadows were long and the yard cats were off on mouse business and Filbert had found his place by the

Great House fire, I crept up to the back of the stable and set my nose to the chink.

I yipped, and at once Comfort crawled over. She pressed her eye to the chink, saw me and smiled, I have no doubt, though I could not see it. She put out her hand to pet me as best she could. Her finger touched the cloth of Alice's hat, still held fast in my mouth. I heard her breathe in sharply, then she hooked the little hat in through the chink. I looked through then and saw her, rocking, holding the small hat to her cheek, smelling her daughter's smell upon it, kissing it.

"It's Alice's hat, Rufus, the old dog has brought Alice's hat," she whispered.

Rufus held out his hand and she laid Alice's hat in the palm of it. He closed his fingers round it. He closed his eyes and tears shone on his face.

Chapter Seven

Summer was hot. The sky was hard harebell blue above our hill. Down on the great meadow, the grass turned yellow and the river dwindled. Water flowed slow and oozy between great clumps of meadowsweet and rosebay willow-herb. The kingcups, over long before the end of spring, set bristly brown stars in place of yellow petals and the water birds grew plump.

I do not much like coot, it tastes of weed and river and feels slimy on the tooth. Moorhen is better, though a little stringy. Neither can match the rich, fat taste of duck. I often thought of hen, but would not take one, in case it brought the village down upon us.

By now Fleabane knew all the country round our lair, down by the river and all about the outskirts of the village. One night of a full, summer moon, I thought it time to show him something new, and took him up into the forest.

He ran beside me, with his brown nose picking up news here and there, his small, neat ears swivelling to every night-time murmur and his fine, feathered tail bent like a bow over his back.

At the top of our hill, rock and grass and heather changed to bracken. A few great oaks stood alone along the margin of the wood. Behind them, hundreds upon hundreds of great beech trees stretched away into the rustling darkness. Sometimes we'd find a clearing, where great trees had died, making space for small new hazel bushes, honeysuckle and foxgloves, their white or purple flowers over now, pointing tall seed heads to the velvet sky.

Deer jumped away from us, leaving swathes of rich, warm scent behind them on the air. Owls floated over, letting fall traces of mouse smell, such as I used to recognize on Humble's fur. Squirrels, with something of a ratty smell, twitched in their sleep above our heads. Fish rose in small, dark pools to suck down moths trapped on the surface of the water. High in a silver birch a nightingale sang and sang.

Fleabane had not heard birdsong like it, so we stopped a while to listen. As we stood, silent, underneath the tree, an old wild sow trundled by, followed by sixteen piglets. Glorious, they smelled. Sweet. Ripe. Salty but soft. I could see Fleabane drooling. He looked at me with only the slowest, slightest movement of his head and asked with his eyes if he should take one. No, I told him, drawing down my eyebrows.

After they had gone and he was pestering me with his *Why not?* I told him how a sow can rip a dog's throat out with one snick of those curved, iron teeth, how once she shuts her jaws on anyone or anything, it's finished. Dead. Piglets you take only if they're alone.

After the sow and her piglets, we met something that smelled altogether less enticing. There's nothing smells like people. Each person has their own smell, as do we. But you can say, as I told Fleabane, that people always smell of more things, more of a mixture of things, than other creatures do.

I recognized the smell of this one easily. It was the rag man who had watched the preacher and counted the people, by moonlight, from deep in the wood. He smelled of sickness and hunger and desolation. His face, when he came into our view, was more than half hidden by an old rag, black with dirt, that he had wound about his head. What we could see – his forehead and the bridge of his nose – looked scaly and discoloured. A bell hung round his neck, but it was stuffed with moss so that it wouldn't ring. He held a staff in his right hand, which lacked two fingers, and he was very lame. His feet were bound in strips of leather, and his garment was a dirty piece of sacking tied about his waist.

All people fear lepers and they in turn dare not enter the village. If they tried, the villagers would stone them out again. Comfort once put a piece of bread out in the hedge for one poor wretch she had seen creeping by, and Rufus scolded her. He said even to breathe the air they breathed might turn her into one of them.

Fleabane and I watched him in silence as he hobbled, lonely, down the path. The path that led to the village.

There were other people in the forest, too. We found an old campfire, and the dregs of ale and urine splashed against the bole of a tree, and bones, some with strips of venison still clinging to them. A pile of feathers showed where someone had plucked pigeons. There were the remains of rough shelters. And the scent of two dogs, one large, one small.

Fleabane wanted to track them. He wanted bones, and company. But I could feel dawn rising and I had a bad feeling about the sick man. We left the forest and tracked him back to Will Cudweed's mill.

Chapter Eight

We reached the mill a little before sunrise. Will Cudweed was nowhere to be seen, but Beton, his wife, was out in the yard throwing scraps to the hens. I could hear two of his daughters in the barn milking goats and one of his sons was kicking Avens out of his kennel to go hunting. Not that Avens knows how to hunt.

Lights burned in the mill where the boys who worked for Cudweed were sorting sacks for the day's milling. It was an ordinary morning, but the place, as usual, was thick and heavy with all kinds of badness. We only ever went there when Rufus had corn to grind. The boys Cudweed kept to work in the mill were always black and blue. Will Cudweed could not talk to a child without a stick. Comfort always said she'd starve before she let Wat or Will work for him.

"Beton is my own sister, but what can any woman do with a husband like Cudweed?" she'd say, and Rufus agreed. Cudweed was the same with any creature. He must be always twisting an arm or a tail, wrenching an ear, yanking and cursing, and always with a stick in his hand.

I sat under the hedge, with Fleabane behind me silent and still as any stone, for all he was so young.

Presently the rag man came shuffling out from the back of the barn, with Will Cudweed behind him. The miller kept his distance and held a cloth wrung out in vinegar pressed over his nose and mouth to ward off the disease. He threw a twist of cloth down onto the ground and stood back, grinning, as the rag man bent and scuffled for it, then hauled himself back upright, or as near upright as he could get. He fumbled the twist open, counted what was hid inside, spat, and held out his hand for more. Cudweed laughed and shook his head.

"You'll get no more from me, you lousy scab," he said. "Unless it be the thick end of my stick."

"'Tis worth more to you, what I've to tell, you know it is," the rag man whined.

"I don't know till you've told me," Cudweed answered. "Which if you don't do double quick, I'll set my dog on you."

The rag man turned his face away from Cudweed. He looked so wretched I could only pity him. Fleabane and I trotted off down the lane, away from Cudweed and his stench of cruelty, and I did not hear what news the rag man sold the miller.

That night, I sat alone outside our den. Fleabane slept within. I looked down into the valley, where the last of the sun lit the roofs of the houses, and I thought of dogs down there who still had homes. I thought of Rufus, stretched in the wet straw of the Great House lock-up, and of Comfort beside him. I felt as low and lonely as a dog can feel.

A howl rose in me and I stretched my muzzle to the moon and let it out, wild and cold, across the green hollows, down to the village, away to the wood. Another came and then another. Little Fleabane crept out of the den behind me, laid himself down close along my flank and sang with me. Down in the village, Filbert answered. Over the hill, Swart called back. Far in the forest, a deep voice, one I did not know yet, joined our song.

Presently we were quiet. Fleabane snored softly by my ear. I dropped my muzzle to my paws and stared down at the village. One or two lights began to glimmer softly out of doors and windows. Smoke drifted on the summer air. People were cooking. Dogs were lying by firesides, waiting for scraps.

And then I saw, down in our own window, a flickering yellow light. Someone had lit the fire. Smoke rose from gaps between the thatch. Light showed in the doorway as somebody looked out. Just for a moment, I felt my hackles rise. Then I was on my feet, barking and barking at the moon, at the valley, at Fleabane, at anything and anyone who would hear and share my joy.

We tumbled down the hillside so fast Fleabane went nose over tail half a dozen times, rolling and bounding and bouncing like a rolled-up hedgehog on a bank, and I rollicked along beside him and in front of him and all around him, shouting my good news to the night as no wise dog should ever do. Oh, but I wasn't wise. I was joyful.

I scraped under the gate with Fleabane behind me and galloped across the yard to where the door to home stood open, with fire-glow and food-smell calling us. In at the door we pushed, the two of us, to Comfort and Rufus, as we thought. To home and welcome, to loving kindness, to fireside, bed and bone.

And found instead Lupus, the miller's son, sitting by the fire with his new wife, Vetchen, at his side. They looked at us and nodded. Vetchen jumped up and kicked the door shut at our backs. Lupus stood up more slowly, taking off his belt.

Chapter Nine

"I thought you'd come sniffing back, old dog," Lupus said.

"Brought her pup and all." Vetchen smiled. "You take the big one, Lupus. I'll see to the little one."

Fleabane tucked in behind me. We put our tails to the door and bared our teeth at the grasping hands that reached towards us.

I heard Fleabane yelp as Vetchen caught him by the scruff and yanked a twist of rope over his ears and down round his neck. Then Lupus's heavy leather belt struck me a blow across the ribs that knocked my breath away and stopped me thinking clearly. In the split second of my muddle he dropped a strap over my nose, pulled it tight so I could not bite him, collared me, and dragged me out into the yard.

He hauled me over to the byre and tied me in a corner there. He aimed a last heavy kick at my ribs and stood watching me with a satisfied look on his face.

"Your master never would sell us one of your pups. Your master was a fool, old dog. We'll have the pick of any litter now and we'll not give your fool master a pot of ale."

I rubbed my nose along the floor, trying to get the strap off. Lupus shook his head. "You'll keep that on tonight," he said. "Won't do you no harm. You've got a thing or two to learn."

It is a terrible thing for a dog to wear a muzzle. It leaves you at the mercy of anything that happens by. You can neither bite nor bark nor howl nor eat nor drink. Worst of all is the fear that you may somehow not be able to go on breathing if you cannot get the thing off.

Rufus muzzled me once, to cut a thorn out of my paw. He took it off as soon as ever the thorn was out.

That night was a long one. Fleabane stayed shut indoors and I did not know what was happening to him. He began to howl round midnight. Then came Lupus's voice, angry, and Fleabane crying out, small but determined. I fought my muzzle and my rope but could not rid myself of either.

Indoors, Vetchen began to shout. "Leave off, Lupus! He's a young dog. Too much of that will ruin him!"

The house door opened and Fleabane scrabbled out into the yard. Then he was pressed against my side in the darkness.

All night he lay pressed close against me. Every now and then I woke to feel his warm tongue working round the muzzle, which had bitten into my nose and drawn blood when I fought it. He comforted me greatly and though I could not lick his wounds, I comforted him too as best I could.

When Vetchen came out to us in the morning and saw Fleabane by my side, she bent, I think to stroke him. But I growled and that angered her, and she took him by the collar and dragged him indoors. I heard her telling Lupus not to take my muzzle off.

Over the course of the day, which was a hot one, my thirst grew into a torment and my jaws swelled up on each side of the strap Lupus had knotted round them. I was forced to dirty all my bedding, a thing I'd never done since I was smaller than Fleabane.

Fleabane did not come out to see me, which meant, I knew, that he could not. He howled sometimes and was beaten for it. I could not even answer him.

In the evening, Lupus came and took the muzzle off. He untied me and let me go. The first thing I did was drink from the trough. The water tasted cleaner and better than any I had ever drunk from pool or spring or river. Then I crossed the yard and put my nose to the crack under the door. Vetchen was cooking. Lupus was drinking the dregs of the beer Comfort had brewed last autumn. Fleabane was there and Humble too.

Vetchen came to the door to throw some water out and saw me there.

"Shall I let the bitch in, Lupus?" she called.

"Might as well," he answered. The beer had changed him, as it does change people, and he sounded pleased with life. "She's our bitch now."

"Unless your father wants her."

"He wants the puppy. Says we can put the bitch to his dog later on. That way there'll be more pups to sell."

Avens, I thought. No thank you.

I put my head round the door. Fleabane lay by the fire. There was no sign of Grindecobbe, who had run out when the soldiers came. But a strong, sweet smell of meat bubbled from Vetchen's pot.

Fleabane still wore his collar of rope, and I could tell by the way he held his head that his neck hurt. He jumped up, forgetting he was tied to the trestle, and tried to run to me.

Humble watched our greeting superciliously from her place on the windowsill.

The meat smell doubled my hunger. Fleabane looked as though he had been fed. Tomorrow I must find food for myself. I lay down and shut my eyes.

I could smell Lupus, leaning over me. His hand fumbled my ears, then patted my neck. I would have liked to sink my teeth into his flesh, but I am not a fool. A dog cannot hunt in a muzzle.

I should have bitten him anyway, because in the morning he put the muzzle on again. He let me drink first, but he did not give me anything to eat. Then Vetchen tied me back up in the byre.

I did not see Fleabane all day. Lupus came out that night, took off the muzzle, gave me half a rabbit, and went indoors. It was a better night, because he did not put the muzzle on again and the rabbit gave me strength. I guessed Fleabane had gone to Miller Cudweed's house.

In the morning I learned why Lupus had kept me muzzled and half starved for two nights and two days, and then gave me rabbit. After his morning bread and cheese – I had nothing – he picked up Rufus's bow and arrows and whistled to me. Had I been anything but ravenous and weak, I would not have gone to him. I was Rufus's dog. But I was hungry. So I went.

Chapter Ten

We crossed the great field, where several families were already working, some mowing barley, some cutting wheat with sickles. Cocks and sheaves of both were being laid in rows to dry.

Most of the men gave Lupus angry looks when they saw him with me. Everyone knew his father, Cudweed, had taken Rufus's house, saying he owed money to the mill. They weren't surprised to see me with Lupus. But they were angry. Nobody greeted Lupus. Nobody patted me.

I saw Filbert from the Great House messing around by the river and he saw me but we avoided one another. I was ashamed of Lupus, and Filbert was afraid of him, so we went our separate ways.

I thought of Rufus, in the lock-up. I thought of the rag man, and as I jogged along at Lupus's heel, head down, tail lower, I knew how he felt – cut off from everything that should have been familiar, forever a stranger.

Gradually everything left my mind except the thought of how to get food into my stomach.

On the edge of the woodland, Lupus stopped and took Rufus's bow off his shoulder. He looked down at me.

"You've got a choice, old dog," he said. "You can hunt for me or you can starve. If you don't hunt you're no good to me. What's no good to me don't eat."

Before long I picked up the scent of a hare in the long grass. It's a strong scent, an unmistakable, rich, gamey scent that will drive you mad even if your belly's full. Empty, afraid, alone, I found it twice as powerful.

I tracked it down into a little dip and up the other side, then waited for Lupus to catch up with me. I showed him where the hare was hiding and when I was sure he'd understood, crept forward, paused, looked back, checked that he had his arrow ready, and ran in. The hare jumped up on its big muscled hind legs and leapt away. Lupus's arrow caught it in the side and slowed it for me. I bowled it over, broke its neck, and took it back to him.

Why did I hunt for Lupus? Because I am not, nor ever will be, truly wild. Because I have known fire, bed and bone. Because I am a hunting dog, a dog who must work with a man. Because I wanted to live, not die with a muzzle round my jaws.

Lupus took the hare from me and cut a little slit in one of its back legs. He threaded the other leg through the slit and hung the creature on his belt. He did not pat me, or praise me, as Rufus would have done, but that night he fed me. I got the bones of the hare and some mouldy bread. No more. But it kept me alive. The next day, we hunted again.

The first time they forgot to tie me properly, I was away to Fleabane. I found him chained to an old broken barrel that lay on its side in the mill house yard. He was thinner, and his coat was rough. He had no shade and his neck was chafed where his collar rubbed him, but there was water he could reach in the trough and he was alive.

Avens bounced out of the barn at me with a chorus of insults. I put my tail up and my ears forward. I lifted my lips back off my teeth. Avens did the same. I went straight for his neck and bit him harder than he thought I would, and faster. He yelped and yammered and I ripped one ear and went for the other.

He backed off. Beton, the miller's wife, came shouting out of the house and Avens ran for his kennel.

Beton went back indoors. I knew she had gone for a stick, but she did not really want to beat me. She was slow on her feet and I had snuffed Fleabane's sweet puppy scent, nosed him all over to learn if he was well or ill and licked his face clean before she came back out. Fleabane and I circled one another joyfully, tangling in his chain, drinking one another in through nose and tongue and ear and eye, together again for a few seconds.

I ran off then and lay down under the hedge, close enough so I could see Fleabane, far enough so that Beton would not have to chase me.

Fleabane, being young and foolish, tugged at his chain and barked and tried to call me back. But his puppy days were over. He was a dog now. He was Will Cudweed's dog.

Presently Lupus came striding down the path, looked where Fleabane was looking, saw me under the hedge, picked up a flint and caught me on the backside as I turned to run.

To run where? Back to him. Back to Lupus and Vetchen. Where else?

When he got in that night he fed me and let me in to lie in Grindecobbe's empty stall.

"That's a good hunting dog," he said to Vetchen, smiling. "Best in the village, I'd say."

"Soon as she comes in season we must breed her," Vetchen answered. "How much will her pups fetch, Lupus?"

"Hard to say. That little runt my father took up to the mill is turning out no good."

"Why so?"

Lupus shrugged. "My father's got no feel for dogs. Took the puppy out this evening and the dog wouldn't work. Didn't find nothing. The one time an old jack rabbit got up under the dog's nose, dog took it and ate it."

Vetchen laughed.

"You can laugh. Dad beat the puppy black and blue. He'll ruin the dog and then he'll take the bitch. Just when I've got her where I want her." He looked at me and spat into the fire.

"Tell him he can't, Lupus! He chose the puppy, we got the bitch. Think of the meat she'll bring us. And her pups should be ours to sell!"

"Do you sit there, Vetchen, and tell me how to speak to my own father?"

Vetchen moved back a little from the fire. I inched away from both of them, but the door to the yard was shut.

Lupus sat up in his chair. A prickle of fear seeped out from under Vetchen's dress. Both had been drinking and the strong, sour smell of beer hung in the air before their faces.

They were young, hardly out of childhood. Lupus, being the miller's son, was used to getting what he wanted. The whole village knew him for a bully. According to Comfort, Lupus wanted Vetchen one summer evening, so he told his father and his father got her for him. Vetchen was very pretty, Comfort said. She thought her looks would buy her anything she wanted. Marriage with Lupus must have taught her otherwise, but she did not give in without a fight.

"Folk won't heed you, Lupus, if you let him trample on you. He treats you like a child."

Lupus jumped up and knocked her flying. Her face reddened where his fist landed. Her eyes filled up and overflowed with angry tears. I saw her eye the knife that lay on the table, but she dared not put her hand out for it. Lupus saw where she was looking, knocked the knife away and raised his fist again. Vetchen backed off, shaking her head. I huddled at the back of Grindecobbe's empty stall.

Later, when Lupus had gone to the ale house, Vetchen found me there. She was crying and I pushed my nose against her hand to comfort her, but she was full of anger and saw only the dog that had caused her a beating and not the dog who might have been her friend.

"Your fault, stupid old bitch!" she snapped. "Your fault he hit me. I'll make him sorry later. But I'll make you sorry now!"

She did to me what Lupus had done to her, cuffing and cursing, hitting and kicking, before hauling me outside. I could have bitten her. Maybe I should have. But I didn't.

Chapter Eleven

Next morning Filbert's barking woke me from my sleep before dawn. Vetchen, in her anger, had not tied me up properly and I was soon away down to the Great House.

The yard was dark, apart from flickering torches. Soldiers stood beside the open stable door. Red light glowed on the dirty straw. Long shadows streaked the wall as a young soldier bent to strike the prisoners' chains from iron rings that fixed them to the walls. The priest stood by. I crept up close, keeping out of the torchlight.

"Where are you taking us?"

It was Rufus's voice. I almost ran to him.

"How should I know?" the soldier answered. "Orders was move. They don't tell us lot where."

The priest's bitch saw me then, or smelled me, and growled. I moved back out of the yard and watched from behind the boundary fence.

Rufus, Comfort and the widow of the man who died were roped together in a line, Rufus in front, next the widow, Comfort at the back. The widow cried, quietly.

Three of the soldiers walked in front, one of them holding the rope. The young lad brought up the rear. The priest wished them God speed, kicked his bitch, and turned back to the Great House.

I trotted along behind the prisoners. The soldiers talked to one another, angry at their early start.

"Why must we stumble down these filthy roads by night?"

"'Cause we was told to, fat head. Anyway, it's not night, it's morning."

"Well, it don't feel like morning. And why was we told? Why don't they see to these rogues here, at the Manor Court? They could have hanged 'em five months since."

"These folk aren't common rogues."

"What do you know? You know no more than they do."

"I know what I hear. I know there is rebellion in the country. There is men marching on the towns and houses fired and heads on poles. King Richard's judges themselves are done to death by common men."

"And what has that to do with these poor fools?"

"They took messages and passed 'em on. They was in league with the rebels. Now they're wanted at King Richard's Court to show the common people what becomes of those who side with wicked folk."

The young lad at the back had been listening to the others. Now he spoke up. "These are good people. My Cecily's mother knows them."

"Shut your mouth young John, else your head may end on a pole and all. And then what will sweet Cecily say?"

The older men laughed and the lad kept silent after that.

The road was dry and dusty. The prisoners trudged, roped in a row, tripping and stumbling in the dark, until the sun came up. The soldiers trudged beside them, drinking now and then from an ale skin which they passed between them. They did not offer any to the prisoners.

Towards midday we came up to a miserable hut, leaning against a fir tree by the side of the road. The soldiers kicked the door open, turfed out a sickly child, and pushed the prisoners inside. They went in too, and shut the door behind them. The child wailed, but quietly, then pulled his rags round him, leaned his back against the tree, and waited.

I suppose the soldiers ate whatever food they found inside the hut. I ate a hen that I caught out in the long grass at the back of it. That was the first hen I ever ate, though not the last.

I do not think Rufus, Comfort or the widow ate at all. They did not look refreshed when they came out of the hut. The soldiers let each of them suck once, briefly, at the ale sack.

I was used to running fast for a short while, and then resting. The soldiers were slow on the road, but they did not stop to rest. I drank from streams when we crossed them, and took a rabbit late in the afternoon, so I did not suffer thirst or hunger. But my pads were sore by midday and by evening they were bleeding.

When we stopped for the night in a wood the soldiers did not untie their prisoners although they were in a bad state, weakened by heat and thirst and hunger. Comfort's face was thin and dirty. Her hair had come loose from under her hood and hung across her face, and both her feet were bleeding. But her chief sorrow was Rufus. He was too old for such a march.

"Can we not bring our good horse Mullein, so that he can ride?" she begged. "He is the Great House horse, but they let us use him sometimes. You could send the lad back for him."

"Only thing your man will ride will be the gallows tree," the soldier told her. "And he can do that now, if he's too weak to walk."

The soldiers sent the lad off to pick up wood and got a fire going. They had not much food with them. Most of what they had they ate themselves, giving only dry bread to their prisoners and a little ale. Rufus did not want to eat, but Comfort made him.

The widow would not, though both of them tried to make her.

"Why should I eat? I'm sick of all this wretched business. Pulled along like a beast on a rope. God knows what waits for us. And God knows why, maybe, but I do not. My man is dead, and I shall soon be. Why should I eat? You eat their pestilential bread, Comfort, if you can, or give it to your Rufus. I want none of it."

The fire dwindled. The prisoners lay humped and huddled to one side of it, and the soldiers to the other, with only John, the young lad, left on guard. He seemed to get all the worst jobs: the longest watch, the shortest rest, the least ale, the heaviest load.

I licked my paws and thought about the hen I'd eaten at midday, and the rabbit, and wished for another of each.

Chapter Twelve

The moon had set and it was dark, when Oxa and his people came upon us.

I may have nodded off myself. The first I knew, Oxa was letting go a stream of rudeness about village dogs who wandered uninvited into other dogs' woods and slept when they ought to have stayed awake, and so on. He has a big bark, for a small dog. There were men and women with him, all armed, else he would not have been so brave.

His people killed two of the soldiers instantly, with one arrow each. The second man choked out loud as he fell and woke the other two. The oldest of them threw down his pike and ran, but I do not think he got far. John, the young lad, was slow with sleep. He stumbled up, grabbed his pike, and stood beside the fire, a perfect target for the dozen arrows pointed at him from beyond the firelight.

Rufus sat up and rubbed his eyes. He took in the soldier slumped beside him with an arrow in his throat. He saw the other, lying on his face. He saw young John, sweating, white-eyed with fear.

Rufus could not stand up, because of being roped to Comfort and the widow, but he knelt up and called out. "No need to kill the lad. He'll not give you any trouble."

Somebody stepped into the light and grabbed the young boy's weapon. I saw that it was Orderic, who came from the village next to ours. We had heard he was taken by soldiers back in the spring, before Rufus and Comfort were arrested. Now here he stood, a free man, in the wood. Rufus and Comfort were overjoyed to see him.

Orderic untied the prisoners. "No offence, lad," he told young John as he retied the rope round the boy's wrists and gave the end of it to Rufus. "Times change, my son. Times change and we must change along with 'em. I hope you'll be a better prisoner than you were a guard."

Rufus smiled and took the rope. Then he saw me.

"Comfort!" he shouted. "Look!" He dropped onto his knees and took my head in his hands and exclaimed angrily at the scars round my jaws and ran his hands over me to see what other damage he might find. He sighed and shook his head at my sore paws and told me I was a good dog. The best. The very best.

Comfort, meanwhile, was patting me and thanking me for bringing Alice's hat to her and asking me where had I sprung from and telling Rufus that if only I could talk, I might tell her where the children were.

When both had greeted me properly, Comfort helped the widow up, Orderic stamped out the fire, and on we went, leaving the dead men behind us.

Oxa made a meal, as small dogs do, of telling me who was boss. When we reached his camp, I saw it was not him, in spite of what he said. A huge old dog, his thick black coat tangled over his deep, dark eyes, rose, shook himself, and growled a warning.

"Down, Serlo," Orderic told him. "These are friends. Be civil."

I crouched down well outside the circle of the camp, to wait and see if Serlo agreed. And what he might do if he did not.

Comfort went with the widow and another woman down to where a stream flowed into a small pool, and I followed. They washed, and Comfort carried back a jug of water and bathed Rufus's face. Then they lay down together, side by side, with no rope biting at their wrists, and slept. I sat at their feet, watching them.

Serlo got up, slowly, and stiff-legged over to me like a bear. His plumed tail curved up over his back and he carried his ears a little forward, to remind me that behind his lazy boss-dog style lay bite and bone and muscle.

I set my ears back politely, dropped my tail, and lowered my body towards the ground. Serlo sniffed me and sat down beside me for a while. Oxa yipped and yapped around us and then went off as though he had important things to do.

I lay down presently and stretched myself at Rufus's back. Oxa settled close to the fire, with one eye on me. Serlo sat by Orderic, listening to the talk. The last thing I saw as I closed my eyes in sleep was his dark eyes on me and his great head, tousled and black against the fire glow, and Orderic's hand scratching behind his ear.

We stayed in the forest for days and nights. I felt at home there, because I was with Rufus. He and Comfort and Orderic and the others were waiting for news of what was happening in the outside world. They talked much and young John listened.

Orderic talked the most. "John Ball, who leads the rebels, tells us that we should pay no taxes to the priest unless payer be richer than priest," he said.

"And he a priest himself," wondered Rufus. "What says the Church to that?"

"Church turned him out of doors," Orderic answered. "He teaches in the fields now. He's a true friend to poor folk. They say he's called these twenty years or more for an end to serfdom, and paid for it in prison many a time."

For myself, I did not care which side was which, nor what King Richard might do about it. My place was with Rufus. But I was fretting badly for Fleabane. He was in danger while he was Will Cudweed's dog.

I hunted every day, in Rufus's company. He shot squirrels and rabbits and any number of wood pigeons, with a bow and arrows Orderic lent him. It was good, so good, to hear his praise and see his smile and feel his hand gentle but hard on my back, stroking, praising, thanking.

When Rufus did not want me with him I ran free under the bracken and drank from forest pools and afterwards slept in the sun and trotted back to camp, to the smell of woodsmoke and the sweet taste of the scraps, and Serlo's great figure black against the firelight.

If I could have known that Fleabane was safe, I would have been completely happy.

One evening, just on sunset, a man stumbled into the camp with one of Orderic's men on either side of him, holding him up. They had found him lying in a ditch half dead of a sword gash that curved around his shoulder and halfway down his back, letting his strength out in a slow red ooze.

There was no point in washing him or binding up his wound, but Comfort gave him ale to drink, as much as he could, to cure his thirst and ease his pain. His name was Ralf Sturdy and he had been with a great crowd of rebels who had marched on the town of Maidstone and from there to a place called London.

"We captured Edward de Cramb, who was the richest man in town, lord of a great house, master of many men, and we cut off his head," Ralf Sturdy said. "And he died like any ordinary man. I tell you, his blood looked the same as mine. It's only riches makes them different. Why should we sweat to buy their ease? Not that he will make any man sweat now, nor woman neither. Not without his head. We set it on the town gate, where he'll get a fine view of all that he no longer owns."

"Then what, Ralf Sturdy?" Rufus asked.

"We made Wat Tyler of Maidstone our leader. And we took John Ball out of prison, who was put there for saying we should all be free. And on we went, with folk running out to join us at every poor village and from every little dwelling on the way, up to Black Heath, that stands outside of London town.

"Oh, it was great days. We thought the world was turning. We thought it was the end of hard times and the start of every new thing. Maybe it is. I'll never know."

Comfort gave the man more ale. His face was turning yellow, breathing was hard for him and his hands shook. But he would tell his tale.

"John Ball stood up on Black Heath and spoke to all the people:

When Adam dug and Eve span,
Who was then a gentleman?

That's what he asked us. We shouted and threw our hats in the air. Then we went on into the town. All the folk from Essex had arrived by then on the far side of the river and the gates of the city were opened to us. By which we knew that there were rebels within as well as without and we were glad.

"Young King Richard and his ministers fled to the Tower of London. Seemed like the town was ours. And if the town, why, then the country too."

"What must that feel like?" Rufus asked. "What must that feel like?" His hands shook as he smoothed my ears.

"What did you then?" Comfort asked. She held ale to Ralf Sturdy's mouth, and wrapped some deer hides round him. He was starting to shiver.

"Why, then we killed. We fired fine houses and we danced outside in the street while they burned. And those who ran out we killed, both rich and poor. Some fought, but not many." He closed his eyes.

"Why? Why kill the poor folk?" Comfort asked, spilling half the ale. Rufus shook his head.

"I do not know. I only know we did it. Mind, we killed lords and priors too, and set their heads on poles and carried them through the streets. And all the foreign scum that we could find, every dirty Flemish weaver, we killed also."

He was quiet for a little while, then struggled

to sit up. Comfort had taken her arm from round his shoulders. He leaned up on one elbow for a moment, then fell back onto the ground.

"And their wives," he whispered, turning his face away. "And their children."

"Why?" Comfort bent down to shout into his face. "Why the children? Who made you do that?"

"Some of the men said that the weavers take the bread out of our children's mouths. And so will their children too, if they're let to grow big enough. They take the work that should be ours. They're wicked, dirty heathens. Some of the men said that."

"Fool!" Comfort spat. "Murdering idiot!"

Ralf Sturdy shut his eyes.

"And was the King still in the Tower?" asked Rufus presently.

Ralf Sturdy shook his head. "The King came out to some of the people then, and promised that there would be an end to poor folk being serfs. But we didn't hear that then. Not our lot. Perhaps if we had, the Archbishop would still have a head on his shoulders. Next day, Wat Tyler went to meet the King. He met him. But he met his death besides."

"Wat Tyler? Dead? Who killed him?"

"The King's men. They drove us from the

town. That's when I got my wound. They hanged John Ball. But the rest of us are spared. All spared. The King has sworn it. And we are all free men. There shall be no more serfs. The killing has bought us our freedom."

"Too late for you," Comfort said.

The men had speared a boar that day. Normally they would have smoked most of the meat to save for later, but because of the news Ralf Sturdy brought, they jointed the whole carcass then and there, cooked, carved, sat by the fire and feasted. Rufus fed choice scraps to me. Oxa gnawed on the ears and Orderic gave Serlo a whole thigh bone to himself.

When all the meat was gone, one of the lads took out a flute. Soon there was singing and dancing round the fire. John, the young soldier, stood up to dance with the rest. Firelight flickered on brown cheeks and the worn cloth of the women's skirts brushed against the grass and bracken, stirring up a sweet, damp scent. The piping of the flute in the still forest sounded small and a little lonely.

The flute played on while the fire sank, and the moon rose, and the young people – and the not so young also – stumbled out into the dark ring of the night to lie together in the tall, green bracken.

Rufus watched it all, his hand curled round

my neck. "Think of it, sweet Comfort," he said quietly. "Our Wat and Will and Alice shall have no bailiff stand behind them with a whip in his hand. There'll be no heriot to pay when I pass on. No merchet to find when Alice or the boys get wed. All that we plant and grow and harvest, all that you weave and brew and bake, will be for us and ours. Can it be true, do you think?"

"It must be, Rufus, if the King says so," she replied.

I did not believe it. But I am only a dog.

Comfort sighed. "I cannot see why the weavers should have had to die, Rufus. Nor their wives. Nor their children."

Rufus nodded. "They should not have, Comfort. That was wrong."

Ralf Sturdy shook and shook, spoke once or twice of somebody called Eleanor, and died just as the sun was rising.

Chapter Thirteen

We dogs went off alone to hunt in the morning, before the men and women woke. Oxa bounced along in front of us, jumping to see over the bracken. I came next. Serlo ambled off to one side of us on his great, heavy paws.

Once we had left the hundred smells of camp behind us, and the trees were all round us, we started to tease out the forest scents. Pine needles. Soft green leaves. Wood pigeon. Squirrel, everywhere. Hedgepig. Musky fox. Once, down among some rocks, we smelled brown bear, and ran.

Serlo found what we were after first. A doe and her fawn. Then the doe smell faded, where she had gone off to graze, and we were left with just the smell of fawn, sweet and strong and growing stronger. We took the creature easily. With Serlo, we could have had the mother too if we had wanted her. But the young one was plenty for us, so we left the mother. We ate and cleaned ourselves and slept. I dreamed of the byre and the muzzle, but woke to the green and brown of the forest, good company and freedom.

I knew at once when I woke that I must go to Fleabane. I thought that Serlo would go back to Orderic at the camp, but instead he followed me and Oxa followed him, out of the forest and down into the farmlands, and it was three of us, not one, who laid up under Will Cudweed's hedge, waiting for nightfall.

Fleabane knew we were there. I heard him whining from inside his broken barrel, but he didn't bark. After a while Will Cudweed tramped across the yard and kicked the barrel as he passed, to quiet Fleabane. One of his daughters came out with a jug in her hand to fetch ale. Another chased a chicken round the barn, caught it, wrung its neck and sat down on a bale of straw to pluck it. Indoors, Beton raised her voice at a servant.

Light slipped away. Night smells sharpened. Dew and smoke, blood and feathers from the plucked hen. And Fleabane, sweet Fleabane in his barrel. Avens must have done something to annoy someone in the house, because the door flew open and he came yelping out. He smelled us and barked, but he did not come to us. Serlo is a big dog and Avens knew it without seeing him.

At last the house was quiet. Hens clucked occasionally in the barn. Goats bleated. Up in the woods night creatures called. Cold crept out of the grass. We lay and licked our paws. When all was safe, I crept out from under the hedge and ran down to the yard.

Fleabane was curled in the back of his barrel. He had no straw to lie on and was shivering. I could smell pain and fear on him as soon as I put my nose round the mouth of the barrel. His two eyes shone at me out of his small face and his sharp little ears came forwards and his tail thumped softly on the floor.

I pressed my nose against him. I lay down beside him, and he began to whimper. I washed him steadily from top to toe. That always soothed him best when he was tiny. It did so still.

One of his ears was caked with blood. He did not flinch, but let me work at it till it was clean. One of his forepaws smelled bad. I nosed it gently and found it hot and swollen. Something sharp was bedded under the skin of his pad – a thorn. I drew it with my teeth. His neck was chafed and there were the marks of a stick on his back.

If Will Cudweed or Lupus or Vetchen had come out to us then I would have torn their throats out. But they did not and I worked on, soothing and cleaning, until Fleabane smelled more like himself and was able to put his ears back and smile.

I put my teeth to his collar then and began to chew. I was two parts through it when the back door of Will Cudweed's house opened and two of his boys stumbled out to pee in the yard.

They had a little competition to see who could pee highest up the side of the barn. When they had finished, one of them wandered over to the barrel, picked up a stick and, without bending down to look inside, poked it into the barrel and rattled it round.

Fleabane jumped up and rushed out, barking. The boy laughed and clipped him with the stick. I jumped up then, ran out and bit the boy, not as hard as I'd intended, but quite sharp, on the leg. He dropped his stick and hopped about hollering, while his brother began trying to catch me without getting bitten by hooking a stick through my collar. He had just managed it, and had my head pinned to the ground while Fleabane went mad at the end of his chain, when Serlo stepped into the yard.

Now Serlo was a big dog. He was heavy, too, big-boned and tall at the shoulder, with a great broad forehead and deep-set eyes. His pelt was thick and black and matted, turning to rust here and there where the sun had sucked the colour out. He'd been born out in the forest and lived there all his life. He was his own dog before he was Orderic's dog. He was Orderic's dog because he chose to be. He could have lived alone, without people. There came a time in his life when he did.

When Serlo stepped into Will Cudweed's yard and growled at Will Cudweed's son, who had me pinned to the ground with a stick and was hollering for his father, that boy knew that he was looking at no ordinary dog. Instead he saw, there in his father's muddy yard, a ghost beast out of the deep heart of the woods. The stick fell from his hand, his face turned yellow, and although I could not see it I have no doubt that his greasy hair rose on his head. He dared not turn and run. He stood stock still, with his brother, who had stopped hollering and begun to cry, behind him.

Serlo, who could have killed both boys with no trouble, merely looked at them and rumbled. He stood between the boys and Fleabane's barrel while I chewed through the last part of Fleabane's collar. The chain fell into the mud and we were away back to the hedge, where Oxa was standing lookout. We were off to the forest before Will Cudweed could stumble out into his own yard and beat one of his boys for losing his new puppy and the other for telling lies about devil dogs from out of the wildwood.

Chapter Fourteen

When we got back to camp, Rufus and Comfort were happy to see Fleabane, though Rufus shook his head at his rough coat and Comfort exclaimed angrily at the marks on his back.

It was late afternoon and everyone was busy. Most folk were going home, because of the Royal Pardon that Ralf Sturdy had spoken of. Comfort was desperate to go home too but Rufus would not agree to returning straight away.

"How do we know the man was right?" he asked. "It may be that some are pardoned and some are not. Even if all are pardoned, they will lock us up again if the King's word has not reached them yet."

Comfort knew that he was right. Orderic

too, and a few others, had their doubts and decided to stay hidden a while longer.

"I will wait if I must," Comfort announced. "But only if we move closer to the village, Rufus. So that we get sight of the children. Even the old dog has her pup with her now and I must be with mine."

In the end they agreed to leave the forest and make camp on a piece of high ground that lay between our village and Orderic's. He knew where we could hide, if we were careful.

There are things dogs can see and hear and smell that people cannot, and this is often true in places where bad things have happened. I knew, as soon as we approached the ruin, that it was such a place. I whined and hung back and Fleabane was troubled too but Rufus took no notice.

"Old dog doesn't like this place," Comfort said. "Perhaps she knows something we do not."

"What she knows need not worry us. I doubt she has the second sight," Rufus replied. "Maybe she smells the autumn coming. Summer's almost gone."

The ruin was a round stone tower ground down to a stump by years of frost and sun. There was no roof but the sky, so they built a shelter out of skins and branches. They lit only small fires, by night, keeping the stone blocks of the tower wall between the fire and the valley.

Orderic and another went off most mornings to hunt. They would steal nothing from the villagers. No solitary goat, no sheep, not even any firewood. They returned each day to the forest, taking their bows and arrows. Serlo and Oxa went with them. They brought back pigeons, partridges, thrushes or blackbirds, sometimes rooks, occasionally a deer, more often rabbits, and if all else had failed, a sack full of squirrels, or fish and eels. Orderic brought other things besides, that did not smell like food to me – wild garlic and sweet chestnuts, hazelnuts and blackberries, crab-apples, mushrooms and honey.

Fleabane and I stayed with Rufus. He and Comfort went out each morning to fetch firewood. They picked up acorns too, as they began to ripen, to grind for bread and porridge; also green leaves such as people love to eat, and blackberries. Each evening they crept out to stare down at the village. On the second night they saw two tiny figures tumbling out of old Ede's door.

What I seemed to see by night in that place puzzled me. Some nights there were small figures moving round the tower. Rufus and

Comfort never seemed to see them, but I watched them come and go, passing right through the blocks of heavy stone. Whenever I saw them, the shape of the hillside looked different. Earth was mounded high into a double dike all round the top and the stone ruin was taller and newer than it was by day.

I am used to scenting things before I hear them and hearing them before I see them. Sight is the least of my powers, though mine is good. I did smell these night people, but faintly, like an old scent left long ago. I heard them too, but from a great way off. All of us dogs could see them. Serlo called them shadow people. He said they did no harm.

The faint trace of scent they left was meat and dirt and uncured hides. They had three dogs, long-boned and hairy, who did not seem to know that I was watching them. There were goats and children and a baby, smaller than Alice, who clung close to her mother, wrapped inside the pelt her mother wore. They carried spears and small bows.

On the night of the first frost of winter, when the stars were dusting the black sky, I watched the shadow people flickering round the hilltop. They had slaughtered a goat and were eating round the pale flames of their fire – which gave out not one breath of warmth.

I usually saw them only at twilight; once the sun was down and the moon high, they would vanish.

This night, they did not vanish. They ate up their goat. Two men skinned a hare and a woman watched them. A girl sat staring at the flames, her little brother dozing on her lap, thumb slipping from his mouth. An old hill dog nursed puppies.

I began to feel prickling and tingling in my bones. Fleabane whined and shivered. Gradually we found ourselves among a crowd of shadow people, all moving slowly up the hill, silent, crouching, hidden from those above, sticks and spears and knives clutched tight.

The hilltop dogs cannot have been much good. The newcomers took the hilltop people by surprise and killed them all. Them and their dogs. Even the small boy on his sister's lap. Even the sister. The old bitch and her puppies. The goats, bleating and running.

I watched. I heard their cries, faint and far, I smelled their old, forgotten blood, I listened to the victors hollering. Then the moon came out, sharp and clear, the shadow people vanished, and I saw a sight stranger than all. Rufus, my Rufus, standing in air, his feet high above the ground. I did not know what I was seeing, then.

Chapter Fifteen

A few days later, the camp on the hill broke up. Serlo went back to the wildwood. Orderic, Oxa and the others went back to their village. Rufus, Comfort, Fleabane and I crept down to Ede's house, on the edge of ours. Rufus cursed and said it was not safe, but Comfort cursed louder and said it was now so long since she had held her children and that she could wait no longer, but would go alone if Rufus would not come. We waited until after dark. Then Comfort tapped at Ede's door and called her name. Ede hobbled out, opened the door a crack, stuck her thin nose out and fell into Comfort's arms.

Wat and Will clung to their mother like two little ticks, but Alice cried and hid her face against Ede's chest. She had forgotten Comfort and her father. She had forgotten me. When I tried to lick her cheek she screamed.

Ede said that news of the King's pardon had come to the village ten days since.

"We could have come down earlier," Comfort scolded Rufus, "if you had not been so afraid!" Now that she held her children safely in her arms, she turned her fear loose against him.

"The priest gave it out in church last Sunday," Ede said. "A Royal Pardon for all sinners who played a part in the wicked rebellion against our blessed King Richard. Told us we must beg God for forgiveness, if we had helped or harboured any sinful rebels. And thank Him for the King's great mercy. Told us God would sit in judgement over rebels, said they will surely suffer great misery when the horrible pit of hell opens up. Numbers of devils, he said, would appear to drag them to the torture and burning of hellfire."

Ede's voice shook. Rufus sighed and said nothing.

"Well then," Comfort said quietly. "There's an end to it."

She sat facing Ede's small fire with Alice, who had decided her mother was not after all to be feared, leaning back in her lap. Wat and Will sat at her feet, one small back resting against each of her knees. One hand held Alice. The other reached and stroked, right and left, the tangled, matted hair of her two sons.

I pushed my nose into Rufus's hand and whined. Rufus was safety to me, and food and justice and all good things. I wanted to comfort him. But I could not.

"You must stay here with me," Ede said to Rufus. "Will Cudweed has given your house to his son Lupus. He says you owe him money."

"Then I will go to the Great House," Rufus said, "and ask for it back, for I owe him nothing."

Ede sighed. "Great House will listen to what Miller Cudweed says. They'll not take your word against his. He says if the debt is not paid by Michaelmas, your house will be forfeit for good. He was sure you'd not come back. He said you would have been hanged in London town if there was any justice in the land."

"What did Will Cudweed ever know of justice?" Rufus asked bitterly.

Ede shook her head. "I told him the King gave us a promise, along with his Royal Pardon, promising an end to serfdom, Rufus. He laughed at me. 'When pigs fly,' he said. 'A serf's a serf and ever shall be, same as I'm a miller.' That's what he said, Rufus."

There was little enough food in Ede's house

and no money to buy more. Half a crock of flour. The end of a sack of dried peas. Six hens but no pig. And no planting till spring and precious little harvest before summer. What could Rufus do but take me off into the woods to steal once more from the same King who had forgiven him?

Fleabane had already taken himself off to visit Swart's farm, where he hoped for richer pickings. I let him go. He is grown up and feeds himself. He was a fine puppy, he's a fine dog now. I'm proud of him.

It was a cruel winter, but we lived through it. Ede did not. She must have given her own share of food to keep the children fed. She was bone thin when we came back. A bundle of twigs held together round the middle with twine. Deep in under her wiry eyebrows her old eyes shone with fever and her hands shook constantly. The first blast of the east wind carried her off.

Rufus took what few things she left in her house, because she had no kin, and the priest buried her in exchange for them. Comfort wanted a mass sung for her, remembering how the old woman had feared the priest's talk of hellfire, but there was not the money to pay for it.

When February was gone and March rain had fed the green growth everywhere and April promised joy and new life, as it does each year, we breathed deep of the soft air, and went to the fields happy every sunrise. Comfort patted her belly, and smiled at Rufus.

She had given up hope of getting her own home back, and set about improving Ede's. Three days out of every seven all the summer Rufus and Comfort worked on Great House land just as they had before the rebellion. The bailiff checked their work, and criticized and complained, just as he always had done. The Lord of the Great House taxed and fined any he could, just as he always had. And the priest damned those few who still dared to complain. Nothing had changed.

But Rufus held fast to the Royal Pardon. "The Royal Pardon stands," he would murmur, ashamed because he and men like him had not, after all, changed the world. "King Richard lets us live, who could have taken all our lives."

Chapter Sixteen

It was the end of summer when the King began to take them. Men came to our door by night, as they had done before.

"John of Stourvale is taken. Thomas Kemp too."

"Rannulf Burgate and his wife Alyssum are in the lock-up."

"Orderic is a prisoner again, soldiers took him."

"It is a plague of lock-ups and jail," Rufus muttered. "We will go to the wildwood, Comfort, where life is clean and green. We will take Wat and Will and little Alice. We will take the old dog, although she's not so spry as once she was when it comes to hunting the King's deer. Which is what it will come to."

Comfort nodded. "When shall we go, Rufus? After the harvest time?"

"Now, Comfort. Now. Put two hens in a basket. Fetch the goat indoors. Put up what flour and cheese we have. We'll go tonight, as soon as nightfall covers us. A hard rain falls when the King begins to break his word."

That evening, as the sun set, Comfort tied the hen basket to Rufus's back. He tied Alice to hers. I nipped the goat to show her we meant business. Wat and Will carried each a small sack, one of oats, one of beans. Both boys were full of wonder that we should be setting out for the wildwood as the sun set, instead of sitting down to supper.

And then we heard them at our door.

We heard their boots and the shafts of their pikes on the hard summer earth outside. We heard the soft chink-chink of the sergeant's mail coat. We heard cursing and laughing. The door crashed down and the soldiers strode over it, their hard boots splintering the wood. The sergeant spat on Comfort's clean hearth and swept from the table the ale and cheeses she had ready.

They took the lot of us. Alice, tied to her mother's back. Wat and Will holding tight to her skirt; the hens in the basket; me padding at Rufus's heel, trying to dodge the soldiers' hard boots and their harder pikes. The goat ran off. I was glad Fleabane was not with us.

Nobody else was taken from our village. The priest turned out to see us go, along with his miserable bitch snapping and snivelling behind him, and Will Cudweed with Avens, and Beton weeping behind them. Rufus and Comfort's neighbour Joan may have watched but she dared not show her face.

It was a long march to Maidstone, where they took us. It was hot, and there was nobody left in the forest to help us this time. Rufus took Wat and Will by turns on his back, but if the soldiers had not taken pity and carried the boys also, they would have been left behind on the dusty road. Comfort struggled on, Alice joggled on her back, blinking her eyes from the dust our feet stirred up. We walked each day from sunrise to midday, rested until the sun was halfway down the sky, then walked again till dark.

At every village we would stop and some poor family would find their door knocked down and their man swept up to join our wretched little crowd. By the time we got to Maidstone there were twelve prisoners, all men. Comfort was the only woman and hers the only children.

The prison at Maidstone was a stinking

place, dirtier than any byre or barn. As we came close to it, we passed right through the market. People stopped their business to watch. Some frowned and turned away. Some pelted us. Dogs ran barking after us, snapping at our heels. I turned to fight the worst of them, a rude brute twice my size, but mangy, and sank several good gashes in his neck and shoulders.

Then we were in the prison, all in one dark room, deep underground. There were fifty, sixty prisoners altogether. Most of them were not rebels and were glad, it seemed, to find people to look down on, people they could think worse of than themselves.

Comfort and Rufus prayed and so did many of the others who had travelled with us. When he had finished praying, Rufus hobbled over to the guard.

"My wife, Comfort," he said, "is with child. You cannot hang her."

Later that evening they brought in a midwife, who looked at Comfort, felt her stomach and agreed that she was.

"What will they do with me?" Comfort asked.

"The law says they may keep you until the child is born and hang you then," the midwife said. "But they may also let you go. I will go to the judge now and tell him you are pregnant. I will tell him also that you have three small children and nobody to care for them but yourself."

"If that does not help, will you keep the children for me?" Comfort asked.

The midwife shook her head.

"Some poor woman begs that of me every week. I cannot. But I will see them safe, I promise you. The priory will take your daughter and the monastery will take your boys. I will not leave them here. I promise you."

"Take them early, if they have to go," Comfort said. "Church takes all, in the end."

"I will come in the morning."

Comfort and Rufus spoke quietly, and lay down together with their children between them in the dirty straw. I lay at their feet. All through the night Comfort and Rufus prayed and talked and wept. They had only just begun to sleep when the midwife returned.

"They've taken pity on you, so they say," she told Comfort. "More likely they fear the crowd might turn against them if they keep you and hang you later. They do not want the people's pity stirred up for you rebels. They'll tell the crowd they're letting you go free because you have three children. It will make them seem merciful."

"Rufus?"

"He must hang."

"When do they come for us?"

"They come now."

The iron grille was opened, our little crowd were pulled out, and it shut behind us. We were hurried up the stone stairway and out into the courtyard. The judge clattered in on a horse, slid off and sat down at a table servants had set up. He was dressed in fine red robes. The trial did not take long. Somebody read a proclamation, the Bishop blessed the proceedings and thanked God for the defeat of wickedness. Comfort's chains were struck off her ankles and the others were led out into the market square. Comfort had time only to touch Rufus's hand as he was led away. She could not see, nor speak, for tears, but she did not cry out.

The scaffold was already set up in the square, the crowd gathered below. The midwife fought her way through the people and took the children from Comfort, so that they should not see their father die. She tried to take Comfort away too but Comfort would not go. She stood still in the crowd until it was over. I held close to Comfort, pushing my nose into her hand, pressing my warmth against her legs, telling her I was there.

She did not notice me. She watched Rufus, with a look so intent, so tightly drawn, that you might have walked down the beam of her gaze. Rufus looked back at her until the last. His lips were moving but we could not hear what he said. Comfort knew, though, without hearing.

When Adam dug and Eve span,
Who was then a gentleman?

She said it with him, quietly. He died very quickly, being an old man, and tired.

Afterwards the midwife came back for us. She fed us and cared for us, until Comfort was ready for the long walk home. She found time for my sorrow too. She would lay her hand on my head and smile at me and call me Comfort's good and faithful friend.

Chapter Seventeen

I could not bear home without Rufus. Once I had seen Comfort safely in at Ede's door, with the boys and Alice by her, I turned and ran.

I did not know where I wanted to be. Only that I could not be indoors with Rufus gone. I ran out across the great field and up over the hill to where Fleabane and I had made a den so long ago. I crept in under the rock and nosed the patch of ash where Fleabane used to sleep. A faint trace of him hung there and I laid my face down on the ash and closed my eyes and dreamed.

I dreamed of when I was a puppy and Rufus would carry me tucked into a fold of cloth above his belt. He used to feed me bread and milk when I was little, sometimes even an egg.

Comfort used to scold him, but he always laughed. He knew she didn't mean it.

I dreamed of hunting and the joy of finding the first hint of game and the excitement of following a trail with Rufus behind me, watching my ears and tail to see what I was after. He used to praise me for waiting till he had his arrow ready, and gentle me when I brought him the game. On a good hunt we were two halves of the same beast.

I dreamed of how the house felt before the troubles came, when Alice was a baby, when Rufus was old already, but content, and Comfort loved him, and they slept together on a pallet stuffed with heather and I at their feet, and Alice beside us. I'd wake at night and pad across the earth floor to her cradle and look down at her to be sure that she was safe. Sometimes Rufus would wake and see me there and smile.

He would cuff the boys, but gently, if they pulled my tail or hurt my ears, and tell them they must treat me well, or else I'd never teach them how to hunt. He would set Alice on my back and Comfort would shake her head at him, and he would boast I was the gentlest dog in Christendom.

And he the gentlest master. I woke alone and sorrowful, and scraped out from under the rock and sat up on top of it with the cold stone sharp against my pads. The world felt large and empty. Neither the sky above, nor the river, loud in the valley below, nor the wide, high dark above offered any trace of Rufus. He was gone. I put my head back and shut my eyes and howled my want up to the black night.

I had seen him, standing on air among the shadow people. I had seen him tread the air again in Maidstone market-place, upon the scaffold. I knew that I would not see him again.

I got down from the rock and said goodbye to Fleabane's puppy scent inside the den and turned my back on the valley and the village, on fire and bed and bone, on love and comfort and belonging. I took myself off into the wood, where the wild things and the outcasts dwell, where the trees gleam and rustle for mile upon green mile with a sound like water, and leaves hide wolf and bear and boar.

I criss-crossed glades and snuffed my way over banks and down ditches, stopped to drink at streams and took myself a fat red squirrel to be going on with, but by dusk I'd had no scent of pig, which only made me want one all the more.

I crept in under the roots of a tree that lay rotting across one corner of the clearing that its fall had left. There was a hollow underneath, lined with dead leaves and roofed with the tangled mat of roots, the mouth obscured with overhanging brambles.

A hidden place, a safe place. A place a dog like me might call home for a night or two. I tucked my nose in under my tail and slept.

Deep in the dark of night, two kinds of footsteps woke me. One kind loud, stumbling, close at hand. The other faint and stealthy. One kind hunting and the other not yet knowing it was hunted.

I crept on my belly to the edge of my den and put my nose out under the arching bramble. A bad smell dirtied the night air. It was the smell of desolation. It was the smell of the rag man. He limped into the clearing, staff in hand, bell silenced with a dirty rag. He stopped and listened, shook his head and lowered himself slowly down onto a mossy tree-stump. It seemed to me, from the way he kept listening, that perhaps he did know he was being hunted, though as yet he could not hear the footsteps drawing closer.

He was thinner than when last I'd seen him, down at the mill taking Will Cudweed's blood money. He pulled a piece of old salt fish out of his pouch and chewed on it. It was obvious, watching him, that he needed rest badly, but dared not take much.

I think even his dull ears caught the sound of footsteps then. Someone was moving carefully through the wood. Coming our way. Slowing as they neared the clearing, coming on a little, stopping.

Some small night animal grunted and the rag man jumped and dropped his salt fish. He scraped round on the ground searching, found it, and chewed some more. Then he pulled a leather bottle from his pouch and drank deeply. The smell was sharp, like ale but stronger. I dare say he died happy, because he was still drinking when the arrow pierced his throat.

I stayed quite still and silent, under cover of the brambles, my belly flattened down into the leaf mould and my ears pricked, listening. Whoever shot the arrow must be just behind me.

When he stepped into the clearing, which was just a little lighter than the surrounding woods, I saw it was young John, the soldier who stood guard over Rufus and Comfort the first time they were taken, the lad Rufus told Orderic not to shoot after the ambush.

He did not come close to the rag man – just close enough to see that he was dead – and he did not retrieve his arrow.

"That's for you, Rufus," he said. "You were a good man and he sold your life." Then he turned, and went away through the wood.

I eased out from under the brambles and trotted away too. I did not want to stay near the rag man even though he was dead.

By mid-morning I had found my wild pig. The scent hit me in a blast as I pushed my wet nose under a tuft of grass and straight into his lair. He wasn't there, or I would not have lived to hunt him, but he'd been there, and no more than a day and a night ago I'd say. His salty tang filled my nose and made my mouth water.

I followed his trail away under the trees and out across a stretch of open heathland, where I lost him and had to cast round in circles until I found where he had stopped to grub up bulbs. After that he went into an oak wood where he feasted on acorns and slept, most likely for the night.

Early next morning he went down into some poor man's strip of field to plunder beans and barley.

From there I lost him again, because he got into a stream and instead of getting out on the far side, he must have walked down the middle for a little way. I tracked upstream and down, both banks, and picked him up again, his scent growing stronger all the time. I followed him back into deep woodland.

I knew that I was near, then, and I wondered for a moment what I was doing alone in the woods, hunting a creature that would likely kill me. But I snuffed up his powerful stench and I remembered. This was to be my last, best hunt for Rufus, whose dog I was still, though he'd left me.

I looked back over my shoulder, as though I might hear his gentle voice, or see him there, quiet, alert, his arrow at the ready. But all I saw were the grey boles of the trees stretching back and back and all I heard was the rustle of leaf on leaf on leaf. Rufus was gone. I put my head down and ran in.

The boar had stuffed himself with beans and barley and was deep asleep and dreaming, else I would never have got near his throat before he'd cut mine open with his trotters, or stuck me with his tusks. I could tell I'd got him by the windpipe, because he made very little noise. But he stood up and threw his head from side to side and me with it, dangling and bouncing from his throat with my legs off the ground.

One of his forefeet laid my side open. I did not feel the pain, but I could tell that one more strike like that would kill me. Rufus's face appeared behind my eyes. He shook his head. "You're a good old dog," he murmured.

"A brave old dog. But you're a fool to try for a boar."

My teeth were locked around the boar's windpipe. I knew he could not breathe, or not enough to stay alive, so long as I kept my jaws clamped onto him. And I knew that he would kill me with his sharp front trotters before I strangled him.

My two strong jaws were every part of me. He shook me like a puppy, but I would not open. Then he grunted and leaned forward, clever, pressing down on me with all his bristling weight. I felt one of my ribs go and the air rushing out of my lungs and a shrill noise in my head, and I couldn't see or breathe at all, so that all I knew was the stench of him and the power and the anger and the weight, and the coarse grey bristles.

And then, just this side of nothing, I smelled dog. Something in the pig changed. He lurched away from me and I rolled out from under him, and as the air rushed back into my lungs I saw his yellow tusk close by my eye and his raging pig eye glaring into mine, astonished, staring for one more second as the smell of his blood blotted out the smell of my own.

Serlo was there and he had bitten deep where the blood flowed in the pig's neck, and let it out onto the grass and with it the pig's life.

Chapter Eighteen

I hauled myself down into the old pig's lair and lay there, panting. Now I began to feel where he had opened up my side with his iron trotters, and where his bulk had cracked my rib and his shaking had bruised and battered me and, behind all that, the dull ache of my jaws from hanging on.

Serlo lay down beside me and began to work on my wounds. He cleaned them thoroughly before he let me sleep.

We were not short of meat for many days and water wasn't far to find. Each morning, I would drag myself down to a still, black pond under the trees and lap the bitter, leaf-tasting water, and creep back to the boar's lair, which was mine and Serlo's now.

Gradually my rib hurt less and my side began to heal. I ate and drank and licked my wounds and slept. I dreamed of Rufus several times. In my dreams I was younger and we were out after rabbits. I'd be snapping and pouncing, swinging their warm little bodies up across my shoulder, racing back with them to Rufus's open hand. Or I'd be rushing in to fetch the pigeons Rufus shot with his bow – fluttering feathered bodies, dropped into Rufus's sack.

It takes time for dog and a man to fit together and it takes time for them to part. Slowly I said goodbye to him.

Morning and evening Serlo hunted. Afternoons we dozed, back to back, our limbs twitching companionably in remembered chase.

Once I was strong enough to travel, we left the boar's lair – and the boar's bones – and each day went a little further into the forest. We'd pick up the scent of something good – a little roe deer, ducks on a pond, a nest of mice, wood pigeons, which feed on the ground and so love acorns you can stalk them while they fill their crops. We'd hunt and feed and find water and rest, and then move on, going always deeper. We did not try boar again.

Each time we needed sleep, we'd choose the safest place the forest offered, creeping right into the centre of a mound of brushwood, squeezing in under fallen trees, once or twice wriggling into hollow logs shaggy with moss.

Once, from inside a nest of bracken, we watched a line of people pass by. They were dressed in green and brown and strung about with game and ale skins and sacks. One of the children carried an owl on his wrist. They moved quietly, more quietly even than Rufus could, and they carried weapons – bows naturally, but also spears and swords. The oldest among them walked in the middle of the line and carried little, but all carried something, even the children, and all were quiet and alert.

I had heard Rufus talk about such people; forest people he called them. They were outlaws, people who had been caught poaching Great House game and could not – or would not – pay their fines, mostly. They lived in the woods, hunting the King's deer, for which the punishment was death. Now and then a poor man in some village or another would wake to find a hare hung up behind his door, or a brace of wood pigeons, or some other gift to carry him over hard times.

The lords and bishops sent soldiers out to catch them. They'd catch some and hang some, but they could never rule the forest as they ruled the farm lands and they knew it.

Serlo and I watched as the people passed. They did not see us, but their dogs knew we were there. One or two snapped and snarled at us, but we lay still and they left us alone.

Time passed and I could feel the season changing. Sap drained from wood down into earth. Leaves crisped and yellowed. Sharp brown bracken spiked us if we were careless. In the mornings, the air was cool and damp. At night, mist hung over stream beds. Soon the frost would come and after that the snow. Slowly, because I was still weak, Serlo took us deeper into the woods, beyond where any people roamed, towards his winter quarters.

When we reached the place, I understood why he had thought it worth the journey. There was a narrow stream and above it a hilltop. Halfway up, a knuckled, rocky outcrop lifted clear above a golden sea of beech and birch. Brambles and holly and dagger-sharp butcher's broom guarded the rocks, which leaned against each other like the ruins of a house. Great slabs of stone, each with its own green pelt of moss and fern and lichen, jumbled one against the other. Hauling ourselves up this giant staircase, we came to an opening into the hill.

Serlo sniffed around the entrance and

trotted through. I followed. Set back down a narrow entrance way, with rock on all sides and sand under pad, was a hidden place – a warm, dry cave, private, sheltered, roofed in rock, buried in the hillside, from which we could look out and see for miles across the rolling woodland.

Serlo's first breath had been drawn inside that cave. His first spring sunshine had shone in through that rocky doorway. His first hunt had started there. Generations of forest dogs had lived, and some had died, in the warm shelter of those rocks. People, from time to time, had hidden there, and left their traces; a bone, a rag, an arrow-head. Bears, for a while, had taken it from dogs and left the marks of their claws in the rock. Wolves had whelped there. For many seasons it had been Serlo's place. Now it was mine as well.

We wintered well there. Gales stripped the dead leaves from the trees. Frost spiked the grass. Snow fell, filling hollows, rounding stumps, blurring and flattening the edges of everything, destroying scent, making the hunting hard. But between us we never went hungry for long. Mornings we ran down the hillside to drink and then to hunt. At sunset we sat together on the topmost rock, looking out over the land, watching the light wane and the shadows wax. By night we lay back to back, sharing our warmth.

We never saw the forest people. But once, at dusk, we saw a red light in the valley and a trail of woodsmoke, and crept down to look.

There was a little fire of twigs and beside it, crouched on a log she'd rolled up close to the flames, a woman sat toasting toadstools on a stick. Her hair was dark red, and it straggled down below the leather belt that held her rags together. Her skin was brown and she was thin and bony, but strong-looking, with no taint of sickness on her. Dangling from her belt were odds and ends of dried fungus, touchwood, sharp white-beaked skulls of birds and small animals, half a dozen snakeskins, some yellow ends of deer horn, a bunch of withered roots, and several leather pouches.

Rufus would have called her a witch. A woman like her came to our house once when Comfort was sick. She gave Comfort dried leaves to chew and something sour to drink. Rufus paid her with two tallow candles and she went away before it got light.

Serlo and I watched her eat her supper of yellow toadstools. When she had finished she drank from the stream and washed and then lay down beside her fire. She had not troubled to hide and did not seem to fear the forest. She lay beside her fire and sang softly to herself, and presently she put her hands behind her head and watched the stars.

Serlo and I were silent. When her fire was dying down, she leaned up on one elbow and threw a few more sticks on it, and then she turned and looked straight at us as though she could see in the dark.

"Dog people," she called quietly. "You can share my fire."

Serlo would not, but I ran forward, and pressed my nose into her hand, and thought of Comfort, and missed home. All night I lay beside her and in the morning when she rose to go, I longed to follow her, but did not.

I had already felt a change coming in my own body, with the changing season. When spring began again and the blackthorn shone white and the streams unfroze, Serlo and I mated. By the time the tight rolled buds of hawthorn blossom appeared, I was heavy and slow and thirsty all the time. I would drag myself down the hill to drink and drag myself back up, and by the time I reached the top I'd be thirsty again. Serlo brought me the first young rabbits, and squirrels, thin from winter hibernation, and dormice, and once a hedgehog, though I found that too much trouble.

When the time came for me to whelp, late on

a spring evening, he stood guard at the mouth of the cave, with his curly black back to me, and his ears forward and his big, serious eyes scanning the distance, until he heard the first quiet whimper. Then he came to nose the puppy.

There was only one. Curly haired, as soft and black as soot. I bit through his cord, cleaned him, fed him, and named him Blackthorn, for his black coat and his sharp teeth.

Chapter Nineteen

By the time Blackthorn had opened his eyes – serious eyes like his father's – and was ready to wobble out of the cave and down the hillside behind me, spring had turned to early summer and the living was easy.

That puppy was a natural hunter; he caught his first mouse when he was only ten weeks old. It was followed by two fat squabs that had fallen from the nest and couldn't fly.

Not long after that he nearly got caught himself. I thought he was with Serlo and Serlo thought he was with me. When we realized neither of us had him, Serlo went off to nose along the banks of the stream, while I searched the beech woods where he'd found the squabs, in case he had gone back there looking for more. But he had not.

I found him crouched stock-still beside a flat rock, his wet nose inches from the fat coils of an adder. Its forked tongue flicked up, then down. Its blank eyes stared right and left, unwinking. They hunt by smell, not sight. It raised its head a little, tasting the warm scent of puppy, and Blackthorn drew back a fraction. The snake uncoiled just enough to keep him within striking distance. Blackthorn drew back again. The snake inched forward. Blackthorn whimpered. The snake hissed.

Blackthorn began to tremble as those fixed eyes drew near. The forked tongue crept in and out and the slow fat coils shifted, slithering, across the rock. Less of a dog would have run – but not far.

I crept around the rock, slow as grass growing, quiet as leaves unfurling. The snake was watching Blackthorn. It did not see me. We were like two shadows moving, the snake and I, with Blackthorn still as stone between us. And all the time I moved, the snake moved too.

I pulled back, drawing my weight down into my hindquarters. The snake drew back also, considering when to strike. Before it could do so I leapt towards it, thumping the hard summer earth with my forepaws, sending out such a storm of barking that Serlo heard me from beyond the stream and came bounding. The snake pulled back from Blackthorn and swung round to me. Serlo sent Blackthorn tumbling over and over on the grass, out of harm's way. The snake, seeing that the odds were against it now, poured itself down a crack in the rock and disappeared.

Serlo and I had words with Blackthorn, several, about adders and their ways. Then we took him back to the cave and fed him on a young duck Serlo had taken from the stream bank.

That summer was a hot one, but the cave was always cool. Once or twice, looking out at sunset across the treetops, with Blackthorn between us, Serlo and I saw smoke rising, and tasted the ashy, woodsmoke scent of forest fires on the air. Once we saw light flickering red, but it was far off, and it did not threaten us. Down in the valley the stream dried to a trickle. Second and even third hatchings of young birds left their nests. Fawns grew too big to take easily. Summer began to turn. Blackthorn no longer needed me, and I began to think of Comfort.

On the morning that I left, I gave Blackthorn an extra-good wash, from head to tail and back again. I took a thorn out of Serlo's ear, and went down to the stream to drink with him. When he turned back to Blackthorn and the cave, I went on down into the woods.

Three days later I trotted into Ede's small yard and scratched at the door. Comfort came out with a child trotting beside her – Alice, of course, but she had grown so much I hardly knew her. There was a new little red-haired, smudge-faced baby tied to her back. She put down the wooden bucket she was carrying and bent to press her face into my neck.

"Alice," she said. "Look, Alice, the old dog's back. I knew she'd come home."

Alice nodded. She did not remember who I was. How could she? She was a baby when I left. Comfort, too, had changed. She was thin, painfully thin, her hair was lank and wispy and her dress was a rag. But the biggest change was in her face. She was disappearing behind her own hunger, her tiredness and her sorrow.

I should have come home sooner. She had lost almost everything when she lost Rufus. A third of everything she'd had went to the Great House to pay heriot against his death. After that there was mortuary to pay the priest. And then more payment to the Great House, for taking on Ede's little strips of land when Comfort's holding went to Miller Cudweed. That left her with very little of anything.

Which little the Great House took another share of, when Comfort was caught baking bread at home instead of in the Great House bakery, as Great House law requires. All this I learned gradually as she spoke of it to Joan, her neighbour, when she sat by the fire with Alice beside her and the new child on her knee.

All that she might have managed, she told Joan, because the forest people helped her with gifts of fish and flesh. But the reeve caught her grinding corn at home in a hand-mill and the fine for that offence is heavy. If it was not, who would use the Great House mill? Comfort could not pay it. Miller Cudweed said he would, from the kindness of his heart, pay the fine for her. Meanwhile he would take her two boys to work for him until such time as they had earned it out.

That first night I stayed indoors with Comfort, curled at her feet, and Alice's, on Ede's old pallet. I nuzzled her cheek when she wept in her sleep, soothed Alice when she woke in the night from a dream. Early in the morning, before first light, I was out across the fields to the Great House warren to catch a rabbit for their breakfast. They were famished, but they gave me my share.

After breakfast we went up to the mill. Comfort went early every morning, to catch a sight of her two boys before Cudweed was up. I dare say Beton did what she could to protect her nephews from her husband's temper, but all the village knew that Beton could not protect herself, let alone anybody else.

Avens heard us in the yard and came snarling out at Comfort; he stopped short when he saw me and I was glad to see that one of his ears was still ragged from my teeth.

Wat and Will crept out of the storehouse where they slept. Comfort had saved them each a piece of rabbit. She told them to eat it quickly so as not to be caught with stolen meat. They would have anyway. They were starving.

Wat limped from an injury to his foot and Will was bruised about the face. They were grey with dirt and hunger and they smelled like the rag man.

Comfort embraced them both, holding them tight against her chest. The boys said they had known I would come back and that I looked fine and fat, and that I must have eaten several of the King's deer, and that times would be better now that I was home to hunt.

Will Cudweed came out then with a stick in his hand and the boys ran into the mill. He looked across the muddy yard to Comfort and laughed.

"Lazy little beggars, your boys are," he

remarked. "Hardly worth my while to feed 'em."

"And I see you hardly do," Comfort replied.

Will Cudweed frowned. "I see you've got my son's bitch whining round you," he said. "Lupus will want her back. You take her round to him. Do it today."

He turned and went indoors. Comfort swore and shook her head. Alice reached up and tucked one hand into her mother's.

"You'd best run on, old dog," Comfort said. "No sense in letting Lupus take you. You go on back to wherever you've been living. Looks like it suits you well enough."

I did not go. How could I leave Comfort? Lupus came for me that evening, with a rope in his hand, and took me away.

That night, back in the byre that had once belonged to Rufus, I howled and barked and howled again. Lupus came out and hit me for it but I would not stop.

A long howl answered from over the hill – Swart maybe. I caught Fleabane's voice and then another from over the next hill, and so on and around, up and down the valleys, back and forth, until all of them gave tongue with me to Comfort's suffering.

Chapter Twenty

On a night when I had seen nothing but the dark inside of the byre for many days and the place stank and I longed for light and air and freedom, I heard Serlo's deep baying from somewhere on the hills and I bit through my rope and ran off.

It was a wild night, a wet night, a night of low cloud with the wind driving in from the west. Serlo and Blackthorn were hunting up on the hill. I smelled them before I heard them and I heard them before I saw them. Blackthorn had grown into a fine young dog since last I saw him in the springtime. They were eating a hare when I caught up with them. I had some too, then we ran down to the village with Blackthorn out ahead of us, jumping and barking at shadows.

We ran on, snuffing up the wet, wild smell of autumn, and presently we found ourselves hunting along the riverbanks. Avens ran out to bark at us. We were old enemies, Avens and I, but that night was different. That night we were the start of a pack.

We ran past the priest's house at the back of the church, and the priest's bitch ran out yipping. Filbert came up from the Great House yard, and then Fleabane was with us. We ran on, seven of us, and fetched up by Miller Cudweed's yard.

The rain smacked down on my back and the wind blew it into my eyes and up my nose and down my ears. It was joyous, joyous, to be out on such a night, free of the stink of dirty straw. I put my head back and threw a long yowl of delight into the hungry storm. It was lost in the thunder of the millrace. The river was in spate, full to the brim and roaring down between its banks, frothing to the very top of the watercourse that fed the millpond and the great mill-wheel. I bit Blackthorn when he ran towards it, drawn by the rush and tumble. Nothing could live that fell in there.

The mill door opened and Cudweed stumbled out, shaking his head. He looked as if he had been drinking, but it may have been the wind that made him stagger. He shambled across the muddy yard and fell in at the barn door. Next Wat and Will came stumbling out. Cudweed pointed to the floodgates on the sluice beside the mill pool, shouted something, then went back into the mill and shut the door behind him.

Wat and Will were small boys, light at the best of times, and lighter by far since they had come to work for Cudweed. They bent double and held on tight to one another as they pushed across the yard, their bare feet slapping in the mud and puddles. Their faces, when the glow from the mill window lit them, were pale and frightened-looking. I licked their hands and tried to nose them back towards the barn.

Wat pushed me away. "Leave us be, old dog," he shouted, above the noise of wind and water. "We have to do what Miller says. You can come in the barn with us when we've finished."

I growled and stood my ground. Wat looked surprised. "Old dog's forgotten us," he hollered.

Will shook his head. "Can't have."

Wat turned towards the millrace and I showed him my teeth.

"She won't bite, Wat! She never bit."

"She might bite. She's Lupus's dog now, Will."

"She might and she might not. But Cudweed

will beat us if we don't shift the sluice gate," Will yelled.

He pushed me out of the way and tottered over towards the water's roar, pulling Wat behind him.

I watched as they walked along the millpond bank. Rufus had repaired that bank time out of mind with turves and clay. It looked silky smooth, slippery and slick with the rain running off it. The water was almost up to the top, solid and hard, like the inside of a flint stone. It seemed to arch a little, like the neck of Mullein, the Great House horse. Wat and Will reached the sluice gates, and bent over them.

Cudweed came out and yelled at them to hurry. It was obvious that they had not the strength to shift the gates, but they dared not stop trying. Wat slipped once. Will caught him and jerked him back before the water took him. Cudweed shouted again and shook his stick. His cloak rose up like wings around his shoulders. His hood blew off and flew across the yard. It barely touched the surface of the water before it was sucked under. Wat and Will watched, terrified. They had not understood, till then, the power of the water that raced past their feet.

There was a soft slither and part of the bank beside them slid into the mill pool. They turned from the sluice gates and looked back at me. They knew they must get off the bank but they dared not take a step. They leaned in towards one another, bent over in the wind. Will shut his eyes. The bank was breaking up on both sides of them now. They stood on a small headland with the black road of the water whirling past on either side.

Rufus came to me then, as clear as anything, standing beside me, smiling down, his strong hand stretched to scratch behind my ear. I trotted over to the boys. Wat put his hand down to my neck. Will held tightly to his brother's shoulder, and walked behind him, keeping his eyes shut. I kept mine on Serlo, who stood watching in the shadows.

When we got back off the headland, Rufus was gone. Both boys crouched down to embrace me.

Miller Cudweed flung himself towards us, bawling, his stick lifted high over his head. He brought it down once on my back, and lifted it again for Will. The next blow never fell. Serlo came round the corner of the barn, growling low down and murderous in his chest. Cudweed swung round to face him, with his back to the water. Serlo lowered his head, his black mane rose, and his lips curled back off his long, strong teeth.

Cudweed began to back away. Serlo crept forward. Cudweed stepped back, Serlo came on, until by and by the breath off the river's rushing iron back raised the hair on the miller's neck and the thunder of it must have roared inside his head, and he was forced to set his heel on the very lip of the millrace.

He stopped there, caught. Serlo stopped too. He had forgotten all about the millrace. He thought only of Cudweed and the stick and how to bring them both down to the ground and savage them. He settled back and gathered in the power of his muscles to spring. Cudweed saw it, stepped back, and vanished.

Serlo checked his spring, confused and angry. We stared downstream. Beyond the millrace something broke the surface of the torrent for a moment, spluttered, and was gone. High in the mill, Beton's white face looked down.

Chapter Twenty-One

The boys ran into the barn. I sat by Serlo and we stared at the water. Two sets of prints in the mud, man and dog, led to the water's edge. The miller's footprints ended there. Only Serlo's heavy prints tracked back into the yard.

Avens stayed in the mill yard, whimpering. The worst of the spate was over, and the storm was dying. Filbert had business elsewhere, and the priest's bitch ran home. Serlo, Blackthorn, Fleabane and I hunted on down the riverbank while the light rose softly, and the church bell rang, and men plodded out into the fields to work.

Fleabane stayed with us as far as the bridge, where we caught three ducks made foolish by the spate, and ate them. Then he was off to his farm, with nothing but a few brown feathers caught in his fur to show for the night's work. He's a fine dog, Fleabane. Serlo and Blackthorn ran up into the woods. I followed them.

We stayed up there, hunting together, sleeping wherever we could find shelter. One night, when the feel of summer was just turning to autumn, we found a place to rest, inside the shelter of a fallen tree. Bracken had grown up through its branches, and the ground beneath was soft. We lay together in a wet heap, and slept the morning through.

I was the first to wake. I felt the weight of Serlo's great head resting on my flank. Curled at my back, Blackthorn snuffled. Something was coming through the wood. Something heavy, with four feet. The wind swung round a little, and a rich, pig smell streamed down to my nose.

Grindecobbe! Mighty Grindecobbe, tripping through the midday woods on her neat, sharp trotters. She stopped to snout leisurely through the undergrowth, found what she was after, and began to chew. She looked bigger, heavier, stronger, halfway between tame and wild. Life in the woods had done her proud.

I watched her on her way, stopping every now and then to root and chew. Soon after she had gone, Serlo woke and shook himself. His ears and jowls flapped as he shook. He sneezed, and sniffed the air.

I knew what he was smelling with his big black nose – the coming winter. Ice on the streams, frost on the ground. Snow and hard hunting. A stream, a hill, a knuckled, rocky outcrop. A dry bed in a safe place high up, with the wolf and the bear for neighbours.

He ran over to the leaves where Grindecobbe's snout had left a fat, sweet smell. He snuffed at it a moment, but soon left it and set his face to the heart of the wood. Blackthorn got up and followed after. I trotted behind. The cave was my home, too.

Presently we crossed a place where Grindecobbe had made a den, and her rich scent pulled me to a stop. Serlo and Blackthorn paused, waiting for me to follow them. The dry bed and the safe place, the wolf and the bear for neighbours, all called me away to follow them. Grindecobbe's scent called me back, speaking to me of fire, bed and bone.

I looked long and deep into Serlo's dark eyes before I turned my back on the wildwood and took the path down to the village.

Serlo shook himself once more and headed off his own way. Blackthorn went with him.

When I got down to the village, I found Ede's old place empty and deserted, though it still smelled of home. One worn-out shoe of Alice's lay in the corner. That was all. I turned and ran into the village. There I met Wat and Will struggling with a particularly stubborn goat.

"Where have you been, old dog?" Wat asked. "We thought you must have fallen in the river."

Will dodged the goat's butting forehead. "Nip her, old dog!" he begged. "Mother wants her and she won't come with us! We're going to live in our old house again. Aunt Beton has chased Lupus away!"

I did as Will asked, and together we scurried down the lane.

"Old dog's back!" they shouted when we got to the house. Alice came pelting out with Comfort behind her and the new baby bouncing on her back. Beton was there as well, her face smooth and serene. I think it was the first time that I ever saw her without bruises.

It was hard for me to go inside the house. It held memories for me of cruelty where once had been such deep kindness. But Comfort called me to my old place beside the fire pit. She told me that the house was hers again, and I, her dog.

Beton had cleared out Lupus and his wife Vetchen and all their things that very morning.

She had swept the place clean for Comfort and spread fresh bracken on the floor. She had put bread on the table and milk in a jug. Two sleek goats bleated already from Grindecobbe's old stall and a flock of chickens brought down from the mill scratched in the yard.

Presently Comfort stopped tidying and sat down on the old bench and wept with relief. Beton sat down too, and put her arm around her sister.

"The mill belongs to me now," she said. "Lupus can grumble all he likes, I shall do as I please – and it pleases me to share my good luck with you. If the Lord of the Great House does not keep me in the mill, I shall live here with you. Will you let me?"

Comfort smiled and nodded.

"I have money enough for both of us whatever happens now," Beton promised.

That winter was an easy one, the first Comfort had ever known. She had her children round her, and food on the table every day. There was ale in the barrel, and warm new clothes for everyone. Humble came back and took her place by the fire. Grindecobbe did not.

The new baby thrived. She had wispy red hair that was just starting to thicken and shine. Comfort said Rufus's had been just that shade of fiery red before the years turned it to white. "The very colour that I saw when first I passed his door and saw him working in the garden," she would tell me, running her hand over the baby's smooth round head.

I wintered at home, with Comfort. In the spring I made one more journey to the stony hill. Blackthorn had moved on. I hunted there with Serlo until I tired, and dreamed of Comfort calling me, and left him.

I felt old, older than anything, when I got back home. I lay in the dusty yard, and scratched my fleas, and let my mind drift back over the years.

White hairs grow in my yellow pelt and my joints stiffen. My teeth are wearing down, slowly, like the turning of the year. Each year, at the end of summer, I think back, remembering all my children.

Fleabane has come back from Swart's farm, but tonight he is not with me. I think he has some business with a young bitch in the village. The moon is hidden behind heavy rainclouds and the night is dark and quiet.

Humble, the grey cat, hunts for mice out on the meadow.

My first litter was of three, but only one was strong enough to live. I fed the others for a day, but I could feel, by the soft, hopeless drag of their small jaws, that they would not suck hard enough to live.

My next came a long while later, because Rufus kept me shut up each time I might have got another litter. He said I should not breed again too quickly. That way, he said, more of my puppies would thrive. There were four, when they came. One daughter and three sons. Fine children, all of them, but quarrelsome, as I remember.

Then came Squill, my small black son, and Parsnip, my yellow daughter. Lost, both, to the wildcat. And two-colour Fleabane, who is with me yet. And Blackthorn, Serlo's son.

I lie out in the yard, listening to Comfort. In my heart I hear messages from the past. Messages of small, plump wrigglers, and scrawny squabblers, wet-nosed nuzzlers, blind-eyed, wet-furred, helpless scraps. Some stay, and grow, and flourish, and some fade.

It takes a lot of puppies to make one dog.

THE TIGER RISING
Kate DiCamillo

Walking through the misty Florida woods one morning, Rob Horton is stunned to find a tiger – a real-life, very large tiger – locked in a cage.

On that same extraordinary day, Rob meets Sistine Bailey, a girl who shows her feelings as readily as Rob hides his. As they learn to trust each other and become friends, Rob's whole life begins to change. Together they find that some things, like memories and heartache – and tigers – can't be kept locked up for ever.

"A memorable, lyrical narrative, rich in emotional insight." *The Times Educational Supplement*

BADGER ON THE BARGE
Janni Howker

"This set of five stories, each concerned with a relationship between young and old, is quality stuff... Not to be missed."
The Times Educational Supplement

These fine stories abound with absorbing situations and memorable characters. Meet cussed, rebellious Miss Brady, who lives with a badger on a barge; the reviled old shepherd Reicker; Sally Beck, topiary gardener with an extraordinary past; the reclusive Egg Man; proudly independent Jakey ... and the young people whose lives they profoundly affect.

"Excellent stories." *Books for Keeps*

THE SONG OF ARTHUR

Robert Leeson

Go sing your Song of Arthur...

So begins one of the most thrilling and magical sets of adventures ever related. Merlin, Lancelot, the Fisher King and Gawain – they all play their part in this epic and extraordinary retelling of the Arthurian legends.

Drawing on the original pagan stories, Robert Leeson sets his retelling in the fifth century, at the time when the real Arthur may have lived and defended Britain from Saxon invasion.

Vividly narrated by the celebrated bard Taliesin, *The Song of Arthur* composes anew tales that have enthralled and enchanted for well over a thousand years.